Also by John Fulker

And True Deliverance Make (1985)
The View From Above (1992)
Chicken Soup, Cheap Whiskey & Bad Women (2000)
Shards, Pellets, and Knives (2007)
Cash, Cars, and Kisses (2012)

A Murder Conundrum

John Fulker

ORANGE *frazer* PRESS
Wilmington, Ohio

ISBN 978-1939710-383
Copyright©2015 John Fulker

Orange Frazer Press
P.O. Box 214
Wilmington, OH 45177

Telephone: 937.382.3196 for price and shipping information.
Website: www.orangefrazer.com

Book and cover design: Alyson Rua and Orange Frazer Press

Library of Congress Control Number: 2015949854

In Memory of NJ—and thanks to
Dick Rice for his encouragement.

Introduction

By way of background for this story—in which I happened to play a major part—I should explain that I have been actively engaged in the practice of law for something over 62 years now, and over that somewhat considerable span of time I have been acquainted with, and/or been involved in, virtually every field or aspect of the profession. Of all the major disciplines included within that spectrum, the one which I have found to be the most challenging, the most interesting—and therefore the most fun—has been the field of civil litigation, i.e., trials, pretrial, and discovery work, and even the negotiation process which so frequently resolves the issues between the various litigating parties.

In that context, it was my good fortune to handle all of the civil defense work in some ten or twelve counties in my immediate area for Aetna Casualty Insurance Company, as well as for Miami Mutual Insurance Company, a local insurer, for a period of some thirty-five years. That chapter of my career, insurance defense work, came to an end, first when Aetna sold its casualty business to another insurance company and then, some years later, when Miami Mutual was acquired by another, larger mutual insurance company. Since that time, my practice has, for the most part, consisted of private litigation for both plaintiffs and defendants, trusts and estates, as well as an entire gamut of other types of legal work.

Insurance defense work for casualty insurers in particular consists principally of representing (defending) policy holders (the "insureds") against claims for the payment of money damages asserted against them for personal injury, wrongful death, or damage to property incurred by reason of the alleged negligence or wrongful acts of their policy holders. This would include tort liability claims for auto accidents, medical malpractice, the manufacture and/or marketing of defective products (products liability) and other transgressions or omissions too fierce to mention. In most cases, if a claim asserted against an insured appears, after a routine and open-minded investigation, to be legitimate, the insurance company will negotiate and settle the claim on behalf of its insured.

On the other hand, if the claim asserted against the insured seems to be questionable, the insurance company will conduct a thorough investigation concerning its merits—and perhaps consult with counsel—before making a decision to allow or to deny the claim. The denial of liability for such a claim will frequently result in a lawsuit against the insured and the insurance company will then refer the matter to its attorney with instructions to defend its policyholder—at the company's expense; and if an adverse judgment is rendered, the company will pay the judgment up to the policy limits of its contract with its insured.

And, because the insurance companies are routinely beleaguered by dubious or even bogus claims, they very wisely scrutinize—closely—those claims which appear to be of questionable merit, and take special pains to discredit and deny those which they consider to be spurious. That which follows is a prime—and intriguing—example of that process, with all its attendant ramifications.

At all times relevant to this episode, Warren and Edra Dickey had owned a sizable farm located on State Route 55 in Miami County, Ohio, about halfway between the Village of Casstown and the Champagne County line; they had owned and resided on the farm seemingly forever. Then, along about 1996, they acquired an adjacent farm which boasted an old, but still serviceable, two-story residence building, located near the boundary between the two farms and no more than a few hundred yards from the Dickeys' residence, and several small, decrepit outbuildings. Shortly thereafter, Warren, then in his mid-seventies, took down several of the decrepit outbuildings and rented out the old residence building to a series of short-term tenants.

In the early spring of 1999, the residence building was rented to a young couple, Douglas and Janis Bynum, who occupied the property together with their three daughters and Janis' mother. Then, along about mid-morning on Sunday, July 11 of that year, Janis appeared at the Dickeys' door and asked to use their telephone to call 911; it seemed that her husband, Douglas Bynum, had fallen down the basement stairs and had been essentially unconscious for an unknown, but significant, period of time. Edra quickly obliged and asked if she could help in any way. Janis thanked her for the offer and replied that they'd be alright; help was on the way. An emergency medical squad from nearby

Christiansburg arrived shortly thereafter, assessed Douglas' condition and alerted the Trauma Center at Dayton's Miami Valley Hospital. He was ultimately care-flighted to that hospital where he died at 7:52 Tuesday evening without ever having regained consciousness.

Douglas and Janis Bynum

An autopsy was performed by the Montgomery County Coroner who described a wound at the back of Douglas' head, and the cause of death was officially assigned as "blunt force trauma to the head."

Douglas Wayne Bynum, Jr., sometimes referred to as 'Douglas,' 'Doug,' or 'Wayne,' age 32, was buried in the Fletcher, Ohio, cemetery the following Friday; Warren and Edra Dickey attended the funeral and expressed their regrets. Edra did have a chance to speak with Janis' mother who told her that Janis and Douglas had had a "big fight" the Saturday night before he died, and said she "was concerned" about him. Some three days after the funeral, both Warren and Edra were surprised when they encountered Janis in company with a man named Mike Warner, whom she introduced to them as "her fiancé." Several days later, Edra noticed that the tenant house appeared to be vacant, and she later heard that the entire family had left the area and moved to Florida with Janis' fiancé, Mike Warner. Upon a subsequent inspection of the house, she discovered that the family had left virtually all their personal belongings in the house; "they didn't take nothing," she remarked.

Although neither Warren nor Edra Dickey ever saw or heard from Janis or any member of her family again, they did—nearly a full year later—receive the following disturbing and ominous letter from an attorney who claimed to be representing Janis:

Daly and Livingston
Attorney at Law
120 W. Second Street, Suite 1717
Dayton, Ohio 45402
(937) 222-0500
Fax 222-0400

June 27, 2000

Warren & Edra Dickey
7456 East State Rt. 55
Casstown, Ohio 45312

Re: Douglas Wayne Bynum, Jr. Deceased.

Place of Accident: 5444 East State Rt. 55
Date of Accident: 07/13/99
Parcel ID: F-10-013800

Dear Warren and Edra I. Dickey:

I represent Janis Bynum & the Estate of Douglas Wayne Bynum, Jr.
We are making a claim regarding the death of Mr. Bynum. Please telephone your homeowner's insurance agent upon receipt of this letter and ask that they contact my office immediately.

Failure to turn this case over to your insurance carrier, may result in you being <u>personally</u> liable for any money judgments.

Sincerely,

William T. Daly

It would be a gross understatement to say that the Dickeys were both surprised and distressed when they received Mr. Daly's letter; this was especially so because of the fact that Janis Bynum had never exhibited any ill-will towards them or expressed any requests, criticisms or complaints concerning their rental property prior to her own abrupt abandonment of the house located on their premises, and because they had always been on friendly terms with the young couple. Certainly, neither of them was present at, nor in any way involved in, Douglas Bynum's accident. By reason thereof, both Warren and Edra Dickey were totally at a loss to understand what sort of "claim regarding the death of Mr. Bynum" might possibly be asserted against them and expose them to "being personably liable for any money damages."

As might be expected, then, the Dickeys promptly contacted their insurance company, Miami Mutual Insurance Group, and personally delivered Mr. Daly's letter to a representative of the claims department of that company. Later that same day, Dick Rice, Miami Mutual's Claims Specialist, interviewed Mr. Dickey by telephone and learned—for the first time—that their tenant had died, apparently as a result of a fall down the basement steps, and correctly inferred that the threatened claim would turn out to be that Mr. Bynum's fatal fall was somehow the result of the Dickeys' negligence in failing to maintain the property in a safe condition, i.e. that the claim might well be predicated on a legal theory commonly referred to as a matter of "premises liability." That inference very naturally led to a discussion of the condition of the basement steps, down which Mr. Bynum was reported to have fallen.

On that subject, Mr. Dickey advised that the stairwell was an interior one, located just off the kitchen, and that the same was well-lighted and protected at the head by a heavy wooden door and a commodious landing; that the steps themselves, some eight to ten in number, were both firm and solid, and that there was shelving on the right side which could be used as a handhold. Mr. Dickey did acknowledge that there was no handrail on either side of the stairwell, because the home had been built in the distant past, long before the adoption of any codes requiring the same. He also advised that the Bynums had occupied the property for several months and had never complained about anything or requested the installation of a handrail or any other accommodation to the home.

During their conversation, Mr. Dickey advised that he had been told that Mr. Bynum was known to consume a great deal of alcohol on frequent occasions and that Janis' mother had told him that on the night in question the couple had been engaged in something of a domestic dispute.

Directly after his conversation with Mr. Dickey, Dick Rice telephoned Attorney Daly, who confirmed that he had, indeed, written to the Dickeys and that the basis of his client's claim was the dangerous condition of the basement stairs, i.e. that the stairs were extremely steep; they were unprotected by a door at the head of the steps and that there was no handrail in place as required by applicable building codes. "And," he added, "the death certificate makes no mention of any drugs or alcohol. I think we have a clear case of *'res ipsa loquitur.'* You know the phrase, I'm sure; 'The thing speaks for itself,' which basically means that the Dickeys' liability for Douglas' death is clear."

Dick Rice, Miami Mutual Claims Specialist

Dick Rice responded easily, "Oh yes, Mr. Daly, I know the phrase, but I'm sure you recognize that I'll need to conduct a proper investigation of the claim before I'll be in a position to properly evaluate it. And, of course, I'll need written authorizations from your client in order to secure copies of the medical reports—and the autopsy report as well. I'd appreciate your providing the same at your early convenience."

Mr. Daly said he understood the necessity for Mr. Rice to complete his investigation and he promised to provide the requested authorizations. The call terminated on that note. Mr. Rice then prepared and mailed to Mr. Daly a letter formally acknowledging receipt of his letter of representation and confirming their telephone conversation; he also enclosed the authorization forms alluded to in their telephone dialogue and asked that Mr. Daly have his client sign and return the same in order that he might get on with his investigation of the claim; finally, he assured Mr. Daly that he would keep him apprised concerning the progress of his investigation.

Mr. Rice's next call was to my office, and finding me to be unavailable, he simply left a message that I should get back to him at my earliest convenience.

He then telephoned Warren Dickey again to assure him that he had spoken with Mr. Daly, and that he had confirmed his earlier surmise that the basis of the claim was based on the assumption that

Mr. Bynum had fallen down the stairwell because of their "dangerously unsafe" condition. He hastily assured Mr. Dickey, "You needn't get too exercised or worked up about the matter; I've already confirmed coverage and can assure you that your insurance is adequate. In the event Mr. Daly files suit against you, we'll provide counsel to defend the action—and if a judgment should be rendered against you—which seems unlikely at this juncture—we'll pay the judgment up to your policy limits of one million dollars. That's why you carry insurance."

When I returned from Court that afternoon, I returned Dick's call. He gave me a short reprise concerning Mr. Daly's letter to the Dickeys, his separate conversations with Mr. Dickey and with Attorney Daly, his confirmation of coverage, etc. We had a laugh together about Daly's *res ipsa loquitur* remark and then got down to the issues. "I'll fax you a copy of Daly's letter and maybe we both oughta check out the building codes concerning the requirements for stairway handrails. Meanwhile, I've already responded to Mr. Daly's letter and confirmed our telephone conversation. First chance I get, I'll pick up a copy of Mr. Bynum's death certificate, take formal statements from the Dickeys, take some photos of the stairs—and do all that other stuff that makes up an investigation. I'll keep you in the loop."

Apparently, Mr. Daly soon tired of waiting for Mr. Rice to complete his investigation. On the next day, June 30, Mr. Daly wrote a letter to Mr. Rice, requesting that the insurance company promptly pay the expenses of Mr. Bynum's funeral; that letter was received on July 5. Then, on July 12—just 8 days later—Mr. Daly, obviously impatient, sent the following curt letter to Mr. Rice:

Daly and Livingston
Attorney at Law
120 W. Second Street, Suite 1717
Dayton, Ohio 45402
(937) 222-0500
Fax: (937) 222-0400

July 12, 2000

Dick Rice   **DEMAND LETTER**
Miami Insurance Group
1201 Brukner Drive
Troy, Ohio 45373

Your Claim #   M0000498
Your insured: Warren & Edra Dickey
Date of Loss: June 13th, 1999
My Client: Estate of Douglas Wayne Bynum, Jr.

Please be advised that we hereby demand $500,000.00 in settlement for this action.

We ask that this demand be met forth with or suit will be commenced.

William T. Daly, Esq.
Attorney at Law
120 W. Second Street, Ste. 1717
Dayton, Ohio 45402
(937) 222-0500

WTD/ads

And Mr. Rice, responded—with what I perceived to be exceptional restraint—as follows:

MIAMI INSURANCE GROUP

1201 Brukner Drive   Troy, Ohio 45373 USA   937-339-0524   1-800-686-9094   fax 937-339-5823

A World Of Opportunity

June 29, 2000

William T. Daly
Daly and Livingston
120 W. Second Street, Suite 1717
Dayton, OH 45402

Re: Our Claim #:   M0000498
      Our Insured: Warren and Edra Dickey
      DOL: June 13, 1999
      Your Client: Estate of Douglas Wayne Bynum Jr. and Janis
                        Bynum

Dear Mr. Daly:

This will acknowledge receipt of your letter of representation as well as our telephone conversation of today in reference to the above captioned claim.

As discussed, your letter was our first notice of this incident involving your clients. We have established a file and have started our investigation into this matter. Enclosed, please find copies of our standard Medical Wage Authorization form as well as an Authorization For The Release of Information. I have made some modification to the latter form, to reflect that we are only requesting copies of the funeral records. I trust that you will find it to be in order. Please have your client sign these documents so that I may obtain copies of the records so that a proper evaluation of this claim may be made.

It is requested that you direct all future correspondence to my attention at the above address or telephone number.   Thank you for your assistance in this matter and I will keep you apprised as to the progress of our investigation.

Respectfully,

Dick Rice, AIC
Claims Specialist

Bcc: John Fulker

At the time, I found it to be of some small interest to note that both letters made reference to the wrong date of loss (DOL); however, the mutually reciprocal errors were of no real significance. Everyone understood what event the letters referenced.

Ultimately, and without further dialogue, Mr. Daly's patience seems to have run out entirely, and on August 24 he filed suit on behalf of Janis Bynum and against the Dickeys in the Common Pleas Court of Miami County, claiming damages in the amount of two and a half million dollars. Paragraphs numbered 5, 6, 7 and 8 of the Complaint specifically alleged that:

> 5. Prior to July 11, 1999, Defendants were advised, aware, and on notice that they had a dangerous and defective condition at the basement stairs which were of such a steep degree, unstable, and contained no handrail, and that these stairs were in need of a handrail at the minimum to make them suitable for use.
>
> 6. Defendant acknowledged the dangerous and defective condition to Plaintiff's and promised Plaintiff's on numerous occasions that Defendant's would remedy the dangerous condition by installing a handrail for use on that stairway.
>
> 7. Defendant's herein, after notice and request of Plaintiffs, promised to install a handrail in order to make the subject stairs safe but failed to do so.
>
> 8. On or about July 11, 1999, Defendant (sic) on his way down those steps fell to his death as a result of direct and

proximate cause of Defendant's negligence and failing to follow up and provide safety measures to make those stairs suitable for travel as promised on numerous occasions.

The Complaint was properly served on the Dickeys, who brought it to Dick Rice, and Dick, in turn, brought it to me.

"What do you think?" Dick asked after I'd had a chance to review it.

"I have quite a number of observations to make concerning the damn thing," I answered.

"And I'm sure you've already picked up on most of them. First and foremost is the fact that it's probably the most sophomoric complaint I've seen in years. Daly has consistently confused the possessive case with his plural forms, almost without exception. Look at the misuse of apostrophes throughout his pleading. Then in Paragraph 8, he recites that it *was the Defendant (Mr. Dickey)* who fell down the stairs to his death. And, in Paragraph 9, he claims *that the Defendant (Mr. Dickey again) lay 'unconscience'* for several hours, was transported to Miami Valley Hospital, underwent surgery—and died." Then, finally, in Paragraph 10, Mr. Daly recites that *"The Defendant (Mr. Dickey again)* is survived by two natural children and his wife Janis Bynum, Plaintiff herein."

"Then, of course, there's the fact that the allegations concerning the condition of the stairs, the Bynums' complaints, and the Dickeys' promises are pure bullshit, and—most importantly, Daly has brought his suit in the name of Janis Bynum, the surviving spouse. Hell, that's not even close to being a proper pleading. Every first-year law student knows that an action for wrongful death can *only* be brought by the duly-appointed representative of the decedent's estate—for the benefit of the surviving spouse and next of kin—which means that the plaintiff *must* be his Executor or Administrator; the surviving spouse cannot bring the action unless she has been properly appointed and is acting in a fiduciary capacity."

Dick Rice was most certainly not a neophyte to insurance claims; a good-sized, exceptionally congenial man in his early 40s, he'd had an extensive history first as a law enforcement officer and then as claims manager with a competing casualty insurance company prior to his having been recruited by Miami Mutual. He was both highly-experienced and uniquely knowledgeable concerning the proper manner of dealing with claims and with the applicable law pertaining to the same as well. In response to my remarks, he nodded his agreement on all counts. "So what do you think we should do with it?" he asked.

I turned his question over in my mind for a moment and ultimately said, "Well, I think you know that I can file a motion to have the damn thing dismissed and the Court will make him start over and do it right—but it might be a better idea to simply answer the operative allegations and set forth the standard clause to the effect that the Complaint fails to state a claim upon which relief can be granted.

"That way we can put the ball back in Daly's court and wait and see what he does next. We can always get a dismissal because of his failure to file suit in the name of the estate representative—and, if he doesn't wake up and do it right before the two-year statute of limitations runs, a dismissal will be fatal. He won't be able to refile."

Dick Rice fairly chortled. "That sounds good to me; it means that I'll have adequate time to complete my investigation without having to rush it and do a half-assed job of it."

"Right on," I answered. "He'll probably wake up—or someone will wake him up—within time to refile, but we can certainly slow him up and make him start over anytime we're ready."

Consistent, then, with our conversation, I simply filed a "plain black Ford" type Answer to Daly's Complaint, denying the operative allegations and setting forth, as an affirmative defense an allegation to the effect that the Complaint failed to state a viable claim which might entitle the Plaintiff to relief. While that procedure was certainly appropriate, it also had the attendant temporizing effect and provided us with all the time we'd need to conduct a complete investigation of the claim and to properly prepare our defense to the action.

As agreed, both Dick Rice and I separately reviewed any and all of the building codes which might conceivably have mandated the installation of a handrail for the stairs leading to the basement of the Dickey tenant house. We ultimately reached the same conclusion: while virtually all the codes which might have applied did, indeed, require such a handrail, the requirement only applied to newly constructed buildings or newly completed modifications to existing structures; those buildings which ante-dated the applicable codes were "grand-fathered," i.e. if the building had been built or remodeled prior to the adoption of the codes, the strictures did not apply. And the Dickey's tenant house was probably more than one hundred years old at the time of Mr. Bynum's fall, and had not been, in any sense, remodeled, since the adoption of any of the applicable building codes.

And, as he had promised, Dick Rice lost no time in beginning his investigation. On July 5, he met with Mr. and Mrs. Dickey, took taped statements from both concerning their ownership of the tenant house, the condition of the steps leading to the basement, the presence of a door at the head of the steps, any complaints or requests received from the Bynums—not only with reference to the stairway, but as to any other matter, the names of all prior tenants, the fact that the couple had only resided in the property for about two months or so, and that Janis gave them no notice that she was vacating the premises after her husband's death. They told him that the property had remained vacant for several months and that they ultimately rented it to two men and waived the first month's rent in exchange for their cleaning out the Bynums' personal belongings and disposing of the accumulated trash, including three 55-gallon barrels full of empty beer cans.

During her portion of their joint statement to Mr. Rice, Edra Dickey described the tenant house as having seven rooms and a basement; she also confirmed that Doug and Janis had occupied the house, together with their three daughters and Janis' mother; that the latter, a Mrs. Jolly, had told her, after the accident, that Doug and Janis had had a "big fight" the night of the accident and there had been a lot of "huffin" between them at the time. Warren Dickey commented, as a part of their joint statement that, "We were really surprised when she (Janis) left just a couple of days after the husband had died and that she introduced this guy, Mike Warner, as her fiancé,—and you know her husband hadn't been dead for about three days—well, three days after the funeral I should say."

At the same time, Dick Rice took a series of photographs of the stairs, stairwell, landing, and heavy door at the top of the stairwell.

Dick Rice also secured a copy of Doug Bynum's obituary, his official death certificate and the Montgomery County Coroner's autopsy report; the latter two documents simply assigned the cause of death as "blunt force trauma to the head," although the autopsy report described a small wound on the backside of the decedent's head. Dick also engaged the services of Key II Security of Troy to ascertain the whereabouts of Mike Warner, Janis Bynum's purported fiancé. Key II was successful in that attempt and actually located him—not in Florida, but in two separate addresses in Champaign County, Ohio. I promptly subpoenaed him, at both locations, for a deposition to be held in my office on October 12 at 1:30 p.m.

One of the more intriguing items that Dick received, reviewed and shared with me was the Miami Valley Hospital medical records pertaining to Doug Bynum's hospitalization and subsequent death. Included within those records was the Transport Medical Record, which contained observations and remarks entered by the Christiansburg Fire Department rescue squad.

Among the items that we noted from the entire record were:

First, from the Transport Report, a "history" provided by the "wife":

Wife reports husband last seen @ 12 a.m., going to the basement to check on a noise. Found @ 8 a.m., carried up the stairs by wife & kids. Wife sponging him down "...when he didn't start responding, I called the squad, thought he had passed out, and incontinent during night. Had been drinking."

Then, from the Hospital records:

Patient Admission: Pt. refd. to SS (Social Services) per Dr.'s order. Nursing reporting discrepancy in wife's recall of events leading to injuries. Wife reports to surg. that he'd heard a noise aft. midnight. Thought a neighbor wolfhound was attacking one of their heifers. Took a baseball bat and light, went downstairs to check. Wife went to sleep. On awakening in a.m. didn't find pt. immediately. Located at bottom flight of stairs, injured, verbal, asking for help.

Wife relates she & pt married 13 yrs, has 3 girls, ages 13, 12 & 10 ys. She is 2+ mos. preg; always delivers very prematurely (at about 6 mos).

7/11:   32 y-o man found @ bottom of stairs, loc. @ 8 a.m. Wife unsure how long. Pt was unresponsive. Squad was called @ 11:15 a.m. (14 stairs) Last seen midnight.

Operative report: The patient reportedly fell down stairs hitting his head during the fall. CT at the time of admission revealed massive head injuries. The patient was taken emergently to surgery on the day of admission for evacuation of sub-dural hematoma and decompression of intra-cranial hemorrhage.

7/11:   Family not available to discuss/approve emergency surgery; will proceed to save his life.

7/11:   Dr. Moncrief in to talk to family.

7/12:   Nurse reports discrepancies in wife's recall of events leading up to hospitalization. Will obtain SS (Social Services) consult.

7/13:   *Death summary:* At approximately 7:40 p.m. this evening, the patient became asystolic. Standard ACLS protocol was followed with no spontaneous heart tones or spontaneous respirations after maximal epinephrine, atropine, and chest compressions. The patient was pronounced dead at 7:52 p.m. The family was informed and the Coroner was notified.

"First I'd heard about her being pregnant," was Dick's initial comment. "There's been no mention of it before, and I doubt that we'll see another child born as the issue of their marriage. I suspect it was nothing more than a play for sympathy—or, maybe it was an excuse for being 'unavailable' when the hospital staff was looking for her to approve surgery. I'd have thought she might have remained pretty close by while the doctors were trying to save her husband's life.

Ohio Department of Health
VITAL STATISTICS
CERTIFICATE OF DEATH
TYPE OR PRINT IN PERMANENT BLACK INK

Reg. Dist. No. 57
Primary Reg. Dist. No. 5701
Registrar's No. 3620
State File No.

DO NOT WRITE IN MARGIN RESERVED FOR DOH DATA CODING

DECEDENT

1. Decedent's Name (First, Middle, LAST)	2. Sex	3. Date of Death (Month, Day, Year)
DOUGLAS WAYNE BYNUM, JR	male	July 13, 1999

4. Social Security Number	5a. Age—Last Birthday (Years) 32	5b. Under One Year (Months/Days)	5c. Under 1 Day (Hours/Minutes)	6. Date of Birth (Month, Day, Year) Nov. 6, 1966	7. Birthplace (City, County and State or Foreign Country) Abilene, Texas
449-59-6058					

8. Was Decedent Ever in U.S. Armed Forces? ☐ Yes ☒ No

9a. Place of Death (Check Only One) ☐ Hospital ☒ Inpatient ☐ ER/Outpatient ☐ DOA ☐ Other ☐ Nursing Home ☐ Residence ☐ Other (Specify)

9b. Facility Name (If Not Institution, Give Street and Number) Miami Valley Hospital	9c. City, Village, Twp., or Location of Death Dayton	9d. County of Death Montgomery

10. Marital Status—Married, Never Married, Widowed, Divorced (Specify) Married	11. Surviving Spouse (If Wife, Give Maiden Name) Janis Jolly	12a. Decedent's Usual Occupation (Give kind of work done during most of working life. Do not use Retired) Laborer	12b. Kind of Business/Industry Excavating Co.

13a. Residence—State Ohio	13b. County Miami	13c. City, Town, Twp., or Location Casstown	13d. Street and Number 5444 E. Ste. Rte. 55

13e. Inside City Limits? ☐ Yes ☒ No	13f. ZIP Code 45312	14. Was Decedent of Hispanic Origin? (If Yes, Specify Cuban, Mexican, Puerto Rican, etc.) ☐ Yes ☒ No	15. Race—American Indian, Black, White, etc. (Specify) white	16. Decedent's Education Elementary/Secondary (0-12) 9 College (1-4 or 5+)

PARENTS

17. Father's Name (First, Middle, Last) Douglas Wayne Bynum, Sr.	18. Mother's Name (First, Middle, Maiden Surname) Wanda Joyce Hambrick

INFORMANT

19a. Informant's Name (Type/Print) Janis Bynum	19b. Mailing Address (Street and Number or Rural Route Number; City or Town, State, ZIP Code) 5444 E. Ste Rte 55 Casstown, Ohio 45312

DISPOSITION

20a. Method of Disposition ☒ Burial ☐ Cremation ☐ Donation ☐ Removal from State ☐ Other (Specify)	20b. Place of Disposition (Name of Cemetery, Crematory, or Other Place) Fletcher Cemetery	20c. Location City or Town, State Fletcher, Ohio

20d. Date of Disposition July 16, 1999	21a. Name of Embalmer (First, Middle, Last) Bart A. Shively	21b. License Number 7813A

22a. Signature of Funeral Director or Other Person Howard E Suber	22b. License Number (of Licensee) 4422	23. Name and Address of Facility (Include City, State and ZIP code) Suber Funeral Home 201 W. Main St. P. O. Box 307 Fletcher, Ohio 45326

REGISTRAR

24. Registrar's Signature Barbara Bugner 25. Date Filed (Month, Day, Year) 1/20/99

25a. Signature of Person Issuing Permit Howard E Suber	25b. Dist. No. 55	27. Date Permit Issued July 15, 1999

CERTIFIER

28a. Certifier (Check Only One) ☐ Certifying Physician — To the best of my knowledge, death occurred at the time, date, and place; and due to the cause(s) and manner as stated.
☒ Coroner — On the basis of examination and/or investigation, in my opinion, death occurred at the time, date, and place; and due to the cause(s) and manner as stated.

28b. Time of Death 8:00 p. M	28c. Date Pronounced Dead July 13, 1999	28d. Was Case Referred to Coroner? ☒ Yes ☐ No

28e. Signature and Title of Certifier (signature) Deputy Coroner	28f. License Number 55188	28g. Date Signed (Month, Day, Year) July 14, 1999

29. (Type/Print) Name (First, Middle, Last) and Address of Person who Completed Cause of Death (Include City, State and ZIP code)
Lee D. Lehman, Ph.D., M.D.   361 West Third Street   Dayton, OH   45402

CAUSE OF DEATH
SEE INSTRUCTIONS ON REVERSE SIDE

30. Part I. Enter the diseases, injuries, or complications that caused the death. Do not enter the mode of dying, such as cardiac or respiratory arrest, shock, or heart failure. List only one cause on each line. Type or print in permanent black ink.

		I Approximate Interval Between Onset and Death
Immediate Cause (Final disease or condition resulting in death) →	a. Blunt force trauma of head	
Sequentially list conditions, if any, leading to the immediate cause. Enter Underlying Cause Last (Disease or injury that initiated events resulting in death)	b. Due to (or as a Consequence of)	
	c. Due to (or as a Consequence of)	
	d. Due to (or as a Consequence of)	

Part II. Other significant conditions contributing to death but not resulting in the underlying cause given in Part I.

31a. Was an Autopsy Performed? ☒ Yes ☐ No	31b. Were Autopsy Findings Available Prior to Completion of Cause of Death? ☒ Yes ☐ No

32. Manner of Death ☐ Natural ☒ Accident ☐ Suicide ☐ Homicide ☐ Pending Investigation ☐ Could Not be Determined	33a. Date of Injury (Month, Day, Year) 7-11-99	33b. Time of Injury UNKNOWN M	33c. Injury at Work? ☐ Yes ☒ No	33d. Describe How Injury Occurred Deceased fell down basement steps
	33e. Place of Injury - At Home, Farm, Street, Factory, Office Building, etc. (Specify) residence			33f. Location (Street and Number or Rural Route Number, City or Town, State) Miami County 5444 E. SR 55 Casstown, OH

HEA 2717 5152.06 Rev. 2/97

"I'm also interested to learn that the nurse noted 'some discrepancies in her recall of events leading up to hospitalization.' You'll remember I talked with some of the squad members that responded to her 911 call. Got the same story; there were apparently some 'discrepancies' in her story to them too.

"And," he added, "it seems just a bit odd that they found him lying on the floor—rather obviously seriously injured—at 8 o'clock, and didn't bother to call for help until after 11:15. What d'ya think they were doing for better'n 3 hours? Praying for him—or waiting to see if he was gonna die?"

He sniffed the air and shook his head. "I can't help thinking this whole thing's beginning to smell kinda fishy."

I'd worked with Dick often enough to have developed a healthy respect for his instincts; they were usually on the money. For that reason, I was not terribly surprised when he presented me with a copy of a letter he'd mailed to the Clerk of Courts for Milam County, Texas—and the response he'd just received. Here's the letter:

August 31, 2000

Clerk of Courts
Theresa Klugh
1250 N. Eglin Parkway
Shalimar, FL 32579

Re: Claim #:   M0000498
      DOL: June 11, 1999
      Occurrence: Wrongful Death
      Our Insured: Warren and Edra Dickey

Dear Sir/Madam:

I am currently investigating a lawsuit for wrongful death that has been filed by Janis Bynum. I have been informed that in the 1990's she was arrested for in your county.

Also, I was advised that the subject went by several different names as well as having numerous social security numbers.

Her current name is Janis Bynum and she also went by the following names:

Janis Jolly, Janice Jolly and Janis Marie Bynum.

The social security numbers associated with her are:

464-44-3644, 464-55-3644, 445-63-0012 and 445-06-0012

Please check your records and forward copies of any and all police reports, arrest records, and all court proceedings for the above individual. I am enclosing a check in the amount of $20.00 to cover copies and expenses. Should there be an additional charge please forward a bill and remittance will be made upon receipt.

Should you have any questions please feel free to contact me at the above address or telephone number. Our office hours are Monday through Friday between the hours of 8:00 a.m. and 4:15 p.m. EST.

Thanking you in advance for your anticipated co-operation.

Respectfully,

Dick Rice, AIC
Claims Specialist

Cc: John Fulker, Esq.

In response to his inquiry, Dick received an entire packet of documents which spanned some 13 years of court proceedings involving an arrest and a criminal indictment for a felony offense entitled "Burglary of a Habitation," to which she had pled guilty. Her punishment was assessed, by agreement, at 7 years imprisonment and a monetary fine of $1,000; however, upon her application, the Texas Court deferred the actual imposition of the sentence for a 10-year probationary period on condition that she pay a $1,000 fine, court costs of $206, make restitution to the victim of her crime in the amount of $1,247.50 and pay the sum of $40 per month for the supervisory costs of her probation. Then, the documents also showed that she had been subsequently arrested for repeated violations of her probation in numerous particulars. The latest order required her to appear in the Texas Court on August 10 of 2000 to show cause why her probation should not be revoked. "We don't really know whether she showed for that hearing or not," Dick commented. "Probably doesn't really matter all that much, but it's worth checking."

"How the hell did you learn about that?" I asked. "Or where to write for the information?"

"I'm an investigator," he remarked dryly. "I'm supposed to seek these things out; you know, that's what investigators do." Dick was not normally much of a wise-ass, but he was doubtless entitled to that which I considered to be just a suggestion of a smirk as he answered.

"Yeah, yeah, I understand all that." I groaned. "Now just tell me how you came to seek this one out, will ya?"

"Oh, you know how investigators work. We peep through the shrubbery, look under rocks, talk to people—all that sort of arcane stuff you lawyers wouldn't understand. I'm not sure I even remember what rock I looked under. Maybe I learned about it from her mother."

"Her mother?" I queried.

"Umhmm. Yeah, probably was," he ventured. "She thinks Janis pushed him down the stairs."

"She said that?"

"She said that's what she thinks. You might want to talk with her, like maybe take her deposition; that's what you lawyers do, isn't it?"

"Yeah, right," I answered. "You look under rocks, we take depositions. Do you know where she is currently?"

"Of course I do. I'm an investigator, remember?"

After far too much meaningless banter concerning our separate roles in the defense of that which we were beginning to believe was a bogus insurance claim, Dick finally advised that Janis' mother was known as Dorothy Price and she was presently living at Heartland Care Center in nearby Urbana. "You'll need to know that she's somewhat infirm, wheelchair-confined, and also somewhat elderly. I don't have any information about her mental condition, but I'd imagine you'll explore that when you depose her."

One of the first things I did the following morning was to telephone Heartland of Urbana to confirm Dick's information and to speak with her principal care-giver, a very articulate and sympathetic social worker named Linda Jenkins, who was quite familiar with Dorothy Price and her personal situation. We agreed that I would subpoena both Dorothy Price and Linda Jenkins for depositions at the Heartland in the near future.

The following day, I made it a point to advise Dick of my having spoken with Linda Jenkins and made arrangements to depose Mrs. Price—and since I had been sufficiently intrigued by my conversation with Ms. Jenkins—that I had determined to subpoena her as well.

"I'll be taking both of their depositions in Urbana," I told him. "Wanna go along?"

"Sure do," he answered quickly. "Remember, I told you before that the more I hear and learn about this thing, the fishier it sounds."

I nodded my agreement. "I remember your having said that—and I couldn't agree more. My conversation with Linda Jenkins left me with precisely the same impression."

"Okay," he said. "We've both concluded that there's something 'fishy' about this case; now define it for me. 'Fishy' how? What is it about our fact pattern that makes us smell fish?"

We were having coffee together in his office; somehow his coffee always tasted better than ours. His upholstered office chair was also more comfortable than mine.

"Well," I mused. "Let's think about it. First off, neither we, nor the Dickeys hear anything about any kind of liability claim for damn near a year after Doug Bynum's death; we didn't even know that the Bynums were onetime tenants at the Dickey place until this Daly guy writes them a curt letter, in bold type, suggesting that they contact their insurance carrier or else they would be personally, underlined, liable for money damages—and the letter itself had all the earmarks of an amateur job; it didn't even mention the supposed basis for the claim or indicate why the Dickeys should be exposed to any liability whatever with reference to their tenant's death.

"Then, as soon as you promise to investigate the 'claim' and get back to him, he sends you a 'demand letter' insisting that we pay over the sum of $500,000 forthwith or suit would be commenced. Think about it. He waited all of 13 days before issuing his somewhat bizarre ultimatum! You and I both recognize that that overly-anxious sequence—coupled with the tenor of his two letters—falls well short of accepted practice.

"Now," I continued, ticking the points off on my fingers, "We begin to hear that the Bynums had argued the night before he was found on the basement floor; that there was probably some alcohol involved; that Janis had at least one major felony on her record; that she had a number of arrest warrants for probation violations outstanding against her; that after finding her husband on the basement floor, she waited around for at least three hours before calling the squad; that both the squad and the hospital reports noted some inconsistencies in her stories; that she was unavailable for consultation during her husband's surgery; that directly after they put her husband in the ground, she introduced a guy named Mike Warner as her fiancé and then took off with him and all of her family for Florida; that there had never been any complaints or discussions with the Dickeys concerning the stairs, which she now alleges were 'defective, dangerous, steep and unstable.' You and I have both seen those stairs and know those allegations to be pure bullshit."

Despite the fact that I had run out of fingers, I had yet to run out of steam. "And now," I continued, "you tell me that her mother thinks that Janis 'pushed' him down the steps."

"Okay," replied Dick. "You've pretty well defined what makes this all seem kinda fishy. Where's that take us?"

"I'm not sure yet," I answered cautiously. "We need a whole lot more information—and I think we'll ultimately be able to fill in the blanks and figure out what happened."

Dick still wasn't entirely satisfied. "So what's your best guess?" he queried.

"Best guess?" I repeated the question. "My best guess is that she ball-batted the son of a bitch and knocked him down the steps. That's what my gut tells me."

"Ball-batted?" Dick repeated the word. "Where's that come from?"

"I don't mean that she actually struck him from behind with a baseball bat. It's just an expression," I answered. "I use it frequently. What I meant was that I think she smacked him from behind with something pretty solid—like a baseball bat, or a wrench, a pipe, or a hammer, maybe something like that. Remember, she did say that he had a ball bat with him when he went to check out a noise."

"You think she killed him."

"I think it's a possibility," I said. "We'll see what develops."

The next significant event was not wholly unanticipated; Mr. Daly apparently woke up to the legal impropriety of having filed his wrongful death suit against Mr. and Mrs. Dickey on behalf of the surviving spouse. On September 13, we received an "Amended Complaint" filed in the name of Jeffrey D. Livingston as Administrator of the Estate of Douglas Wayne Bynum, Jr., Deceased. We had already discussed the fact that this was the proper way to bring the action, i.e. in the name of a duly appointed representative of the decedent's estate. I was nonetheless surprised that he had not secured Janis' appointment as the estate representative instead of one Jeffrey D. Livingston— whom I believed to be an attorney associated with Mr. Daly. I later concluded that he had done so because Mr. Livingston was more likely to be available for purposes of court proceedings. I also noted that—inappropriately and unnecessarily, but of no practical significance—he also named Janis Bynum as a co-plaintiff, along with Mr. Livingston.

Meanwhile, on the afternoon of October 31, Michael Dean Warner (Janis' fiancé) appeared in my offices for the purpose of my taking his deposition—as upon cross-examination—pursuant to the subpoena I had caused to be served on him earlier. And, of course, Dick Rice was also on hand for that event.

Although Dick had told me that Mike Warner was nicknamed "Buckethead" because his head was perceived to be inordinately large, he nonetheless impressed me as a well-kempt, good-looking young man who showed no resentment about being required to appear and answer pursuant to subpoena. He struck me as quite amiable and seemed to be both truthful and candid in his answers to my questions. Some of his responses were at odds with information that we'd already developed, but I was quite certain that his answers, if perhaps imprecise, were in accordance with his best recollection; he did, however, have some difficulty in remembering specific names, dates and places with reference to events that had transpired more than a year earlier.

He told me that he currently resided on Terre Haute Road, Urbana, Ohio, along with his two sons by a marriage which had terminated in a divorce some eight years earlier; he and his ex-wife had shared custody of the two boys. He was exactly 10 days shy of his 41st birthday, unmarried and was currently employed through an employment service as a maintenance person at the Honeywell plant in Urbana for the past six months. He also owned and operated a used furniture store in Urbana. He was a high school graduate, with no further schooling and no criminal record.

In response to my questioning, he said that he'd met Janis Bynum several months before her husband died. On several occasions she'd come to his used furniture store and had bought several items from him. On the day of her husband's funeral, she'd stopped at his store and told him her husband had died. "He fell down the stairs, the only thing she told me at that time."

Although he said he hadn't gone to the funeral and had never heard her refer to him as her fiancé, he did tell me that about a week after the funeral, she'd come to his store and bought a used washer from him; and, because the washer needed repair, he promised to fix it and deliver it to her home (the Dickey tenant house) the following day. When he did so, he said they'd spent some time together, "probably two hours," talking and helping her daughter get her car running. And though they became friendly, saw each other "probably every other day" and went out to dinner together, he denied having sexual relations with her until "a month, month and a half" after the funeral. From that time on, they'd seen one another—and had sexual relations together "about every other day"—at the Dickey home, at his furniture store and once in a vehicle. He said they hadn't used any kind of protection because, "She said she can't get pregnant 'cause she's been fixed or something."

Contrary to what the Dickeys had told us, Mike Warner indicated that he and Janis had lived together at the Dickey place for a considerable period of time after the funeral. Then, when they finally left for Florida sometime in October or November, she left virtually everything in the house but her clothes.

In response to my specific questions, he acknowledged that the two of them, together with Janis' three kids and her mother, went to Florida, "right before winter to pick up her brother." As it happened, however, her brother wasn't at the trailer court where Janis thought he would be. After making a few telephone inquiries over the next few days, she managed to locate him and agreed to pick him up on the way back to Ohio—somewhere south of Kentucky, "probably in Tennessee."

Although the original purpose of the trip was supposed to be to bring her brother back to Ohio, it developed during the testimony that the real plan was to dump Janis' mother on him and return without either her brother or her mother. Unhappily for them, her brother, whose name Mike Warner couldn't remember, turned out to be homeless, so both he and their mother rode back to Ohio with Mike, Janis and the three kids. They arrived sometime in November and the entire group took up residence at Kiser Lake State Park in Champaign County, where they lived in three tents by day and slept in a van at night. During the entire time of their residence at the state park, Mike said he drove to Urbana every day to run his store and Janis would leave the kids in the care of her mother and brother. That routine lasted until the Champaign County authorities got into the act. When Mike and Janis returned from an auction one evening they found a note pinned on one of the tents. It seems that the county sheriff had evicted Janis' brother, delivered the kids to the Children's Protective Agency and taken Janis' mother, who was ill, to the hospital. The sheriff's note also advised that they could not continue to live in that fashion in the State Park—and that they should contact his office immediately.

After conferring with the sheriff, they took down the tents that same evening, and with the sheriff's permission—since they had no other place to go—Mike and Janis spent the balance of that night and one or two more in the van which was still located in the park. They next stayed for a short period in Mike's store. Then, because Champaign County Children's Services had placed the three kids in a foster home and refused to release them to Janis until and unless she found more suitable quarters, she managed to rent an apartment on Terre Haute Road, Urbana, and Janis moved into that home, along with Mike and the three girls shortly before Christmas. Her mother had been released from the hospital and transferred to Heartland Care Center, and her brother had apparently drifted back to Tennessee.

Then, a few days after Christmas, December 29 or 30, Mike moved out for good.

"Why did you happen to move out?" I asked.

"Cause me and her were fighting," he answered.

And, at a later point in the deposition, Mike and I had an intriguing dialogue:

Q During the time the two of you were living together and seeing one another, did you have quarrels?

A You mean fights?

Q Yeah.

A I don't hit women.

Q Okay, did you have disagreements?

A   Yeah.

Q   Did she get pretty intense?

A   Yeah. Couple times.

Q   Did she ever physically attack you?

A   She tried to stab me two times with a knife.

Q   Let's talk about these. When was the first time she tried to stab you with a knife?

A   That's been so long, I can't remember.

Q   Do the best you can.

A   I was arguing about Matt, the guy she was seeing. She said she wasn't seeing him. I told her, I said, "Janis, you lied to me."

Q   You said that?

A   Yeah. I told her, "You know you lie"—I said, "You lie to your daughters and stuff."

Q   Did that make her angry?

A   Yeah.

Q   Is that when she took the knife and attacked you?

A   Once.

Q   What kind of knife was it?

A   Kitchen knife.

Q   Steak knife or butter knife?

A   Yeah, steak knife. She came straight to me and pointed the knife in my belly first time she did it.

Q   Did she manage to nick you?

A   Nope.

Q   Did you catch her arm or her hand? How did you avoid being stabbed?

A   I told her, "Keep the knife away from me."

Q   Was that enough?

A   After a couple of minutes it was. I told her I was going to call the sheriff on her.

Q   But she was actually threatening you with the knife?

A   Mm-hmm.

Q   Was there another time?

A   Yep.

Q   How long after that?

A   About a month later.

Q   What was that about?

A   Same—about the same thing.

Q   She come at you with the knife again?

A   Yeah.

Q   Same way?

A   Yep.

Q   Just brandish it?

A   Yep.

Q   She didn't touch you with it?

A   Almost.

Q   She tried?

A   Yeah.

Q   And, what, you got out of the way?

A   Yeah. I said, "Put the knife up."

Q   You didn't have to stop her physically?

A   No. She said—she told me, "Hey, I done it once. I can do it again."

Q   What was it she said she had done once?

A   She said she killed one person, she can do the same way again, kill somebody again.

Q   What did you understand her to mean by that?

A   The only thing I thought she meant by it was she killed her husband.

Q   Was that Wayne Douglas Bynum or Douglas Wayne Bynum?

A   Mm-hmm.

Q   We talked earlier about when she told you that her husband fell down the stairs. Did you ever have any other conversations with her about how her husband died?

A   No. Her mom told me that Janis killed him.

Q   Janis' mother said that Janis killed her husband?

A   (Nodding in the affirmative.) Her mom told me that both of them were drunk one night and they were fighting.

Q   Was her mom in the house at that time?

A   She was in bed that night.

Q   In the house?

A   Yeah.

Q   And that night, had she heard them arguing, did she tell you?

A   Before they went to bed they was arguing.

At that point in my examination, I shifted gears, paused as if to study my notes, shot a mischievous glance at Dick Rice, (I think God made me do it), and asked (almost facetiously):

Q   Was there any mention of a ball bat?

A   Yeah.

Q   Who mentioned the ball bat?

A I heard the sheriff's department—I know the Champaign County Sheriff's guys. I know them guys, and they told me what happened. They said they think Janis hit—

Q The deputies at the sheriff's office said that?

A Yeah.

Q Did they indicate why they thought that?

A They found a baseball bat down the stairs. They said they can't take prints off baseball bats 'cause prints mess up on baseball bats or something, smudge.

Q Was this supposed to be a wooden bat or an aluminum bat?

A Wooden bat.

Q Which was found at the bottom of the steps?

A Yeah.

Q Did it have a grip on the handle, tape or rubber, or was it just a naked bat?

A It was a wooden bat. It didn't have no tape or nothing on it. It was a regular bat.

Although Mike Warner had earlier denied that Janis had introduced him to anyone as her fiancé, he freely admitted that they had initially intended to get married. That would have been in October or November. In response to my further questions as to why they had not done so, he simply said:

A I didn't trust her at all.

Q From what standpoint did you not trust her? You didn't trust her to be faithful to you? You didn't trust her to tell you the truth?

A   Both.

Q   Had she given you some reason not to trust her?

A   I heard she was seeing another guy.

Q   At the same time she was seeing you.

A   Yeah. Matt something—he lives in the town of Thackery.

Mike Warner's deposition was concluded just before 3 o'clock and he was excused with my thanks for his co-operation. Then, after Susan Bickert, the court reporter, had packed up her stenographic equipment and departed, Dick and I settled back to reprise and evaluate his testimony. The coffee pot was still about half full and it seemed a shame to waste the rest. Besides, we wanted to discuss what he'd told us and to compare that with what we'd already heard from other sources.

"Were you surprised that neither Mr. Daly nor anyone else on his behalf appeared for the deposition?" I asked. "I filed a Notice of Taking with the Court and served him with a copy. I should have thought he'd have wanted to be here."

"What's that tell you?" Dick asked.

"It *suggests* to me that because you didn't send him a check for $500,000 when he demanded it last July it might have occurred to him that maybe it wasn't just going to appear under his pillow one morning," I answered. "It's like he never thought that he just might have to go to trial and prove his case."

"You mean you think he's losing his faith in the tooth fairy?"

"Well, I think he still has high hopes," I said. "But the extent of that faith may be wavering a bit."

Then we turned our attention to Mike Warner's testimony.

"Does it bother you at all that the story we just heard doesn't quite tally with what the Dickeys told us about Janis' having left right after the funeral and their never having seen her again?" Dick asked by way of beginning our discussion.

"Not really," I answered. "We're talking about a sequence of events that happened more than a year ago, and I doubt if anybody was keeping time records. I expect that all of them believe what they've told us on that score. By the same token, I believe that Mike Warner never heard Janis introduce him as her fiancé. I'm inclined to believe that Mrs. Dickey may have referred to him that way in a conversation she had with him at some later time and that the Dickeys have somehow convinced themselves that she introduced him to them in that context. We both know how the passage of time can distort peoples' memories. That'd be especially true of the Dickeys, both of whom are quite elderly."

Dick nodded his agreement. "I think you're right on that score. If everybody we talked with agreed precisely about everything that had happened that long ago, I'd be convinced that they were all lying to us."

"And," I added, "What difference does it make anyway? We've pretty well established that there came a time—either before or after Doug Bynum's death—when a romantic relationship developed between Janis and this Warner guy; that they intended to get married and that the whole passel of them went to Florida, etc., etc., pretty much what Mike Warner just told us. And, more to the point, we learned a great deal about Janis Bynum's history and her temperament."

"Um-hmm," Dick said wryly. "We sure did. We learned a lot of things. We even learned about a ball bat found at the scene, didn't we?"

I knew I would hear about that. "Honest Indian, Dick. Scout's honor, I guarantee that that was a total shot in the dark. I only asked the question—facetiously—because of our earlier discussion. I was more surprised than you were when I heard that there was actually a ball bat found at the scene and that the Champaign Sheriff's Deputies had speculated about its being a murder weapon."

"Um-hmm, 'just an expression,' I think you said." He grimaced at me and rubbed his eyes. "Oh Lord," he intoned. "When will I ever learn you should never trust a lawyer, not even your own?"

I continued to protest my innocence—as well as my ignorance of the existence of a ball bat—but I doubt that he'll ever believe me. I stand, nevertheless, on my assurance that I had used the phraseology as nothing more nor less than a form of expression, a fortuitous idiom.

It seemed like a good time to change the subject. "How come I haven't heard from you on the subject of Janis' mother's age? I'm sure you know I didn't like that much," I remarked.

"Didn't like what much?" he asked with mock sincerity.

"You know damned good and well what I'm talking about," I snorted.

"Oh," he replied. "You mean when you asked how old Janis' mother was?"

"That's what I'm talking about…"

"Yeah, that's it. And he said she was really old. Then you tried to nail it down and asked if she appeared to be as old as you were." He couldn't resist a chuckle, "and he said 'no, not that old.' Yeah, I seem to remember that."

"Um-hmm," I conceded dourly. "Me, too."

Along about this time, I became convinced that Dick Rice never slept—at least while he had an active case pending. On November 2, I received a fax transmission from him in which he advised that he had telephoned the local police departments in both Belton and Temple, Texas, and the Bell County Sheriffs' Department. All of those departments, he reported, were well-acquainted with both Janis and Douglas Bynum. He was told that Douglas was a known alcoholic and had served time for breaking and entering, and there were, at that time, three outstanding warrants for his arrest. Dick told them that they could forget about the outstanding warrants for the very good reason that he was now deceased.

Along about the same time, early November, I had served on Mr. Daly a set of Written Interrogatories to Plaintiff Janis Bynum, along with a Request for Production of Documents, and filed a formal Notice to that effect with the Court. A formal response to those interrogatories and the request for production was due within 28 days thereafter.

The next order of business with reference to the wrongful death action initiated by Mr. Daly against the Dickeys took Dick and I to Heartland of Urbana Care Center on November 17 of 2000 for the scheduled depositions of Dorothy Price and Linda Jenkins. On the morning of that day, I received both a fax communique and an ordinary, mailed letter from Mr. Daly asking that the depositions be continued to a later date because he had a prior commitment that would prevent him from attending. In connection with his request, he failed to acknowledge the fact that the Notice of those two depositions had been sent to him eight days earlier, on the 9th of November. By way of response I faxed him a letter pointing out that I could not defer the deposition of Dorothy Price because she was scheduled to be moved to Texas before the end of the month.

"So what do we do now?" asked Dick Rice.

"We proceed as planned," I answered. "If he truly had a prior commitment, he had ample time to telephone long before today. Had he done so, I might have been inclined to reschedule, but I'm sure as hell not going to do so now."

"Can he prevent us from proceeding—or get an order preventing us from proceeding?" asked Dick.

"No way," I responded. "He had ample notice and waited 'till today to request a continuance. The Rules are clear. Besides, he can find someone to attend in his place if he chooses. Remember, he made no attempt to attend Mike Warner's deposition."

And, of course, we heard no more about it, and no one appeared on behalf of the Plaintiff.

The first of the two depositions was that of Janis Bynum's mother, who impressed me as quite frail, but both candid and reasonably cogent; I found a measure of relief in that respect because Dick Rice had taken her taped statement earlier and shared with me his opinion that she might not have been fully competent. She dispelled that impression rather promptly when she gave her name as Dorothy Bell Price, her birth date as July 16, 1942, and her residence at the Heartland nursing home in Urbana, Ohio. In response to my questions, she told me that she had been born in Junction, Texas, and had been married at age 16 to Junior Jolly; that the two of them had had five children, four girls and a boy, all of whom she listed by name. She said that her marriage to Junior Jolly had lasted 19 years and was terminated in divorce, and that she thereafter married Walter Price on the 19th of October, but wasn't sure of the year. There were no children of that marriage, and he had died "about a year ago."

When I asked her whether there was a time when she resided with her daughter Janis and Douglas Bynum, she told me that the two of them had come to a nursing home in Kansas where she and her husband were living and brought the two of them to Urbana to live with them:

Q Was that at your request?

A No.

Q Do you know why they did that?

A 'Cause they wanted my money.

Q   Okay. And are we referring to a Social Security check or pension check or—

A   Social Security.

She said they brought her to a house they'd occupied in Urbana, but then later they all moved to the Dickey farm. When I asked her why they had moved from Urbana to the Dickey farm, she indicated it was because they couldn't pay the rent. Because she wasn't sure how long they had resided on the Dickey farm before Douglas had died, she was unable to answer definitively. She first said "pretty good while." Then, when I pressed, she guessed it had been "almost a year." On the other hand, she was able to identify, without any prompting on my part, all of the members of Doug and Janis' menage; she named all of their children and provided their approximate ages. She even volunteered the fact that only the younger two were the issue of their marriage; the eldest daughter, Amanda, had been the product of Janis' first marriage to a man whose name she couldn't say because she'd never met him, and their marriage hadn't lasted very long. She said that very soon after Amanda had been born, probably 13 or 14 years ago, Janis had married Douglas Bynum and the two of them were raising all the girls as their own.

When I asked if she knew where Janis and the children were at that time, she said, "Well, she told everybody she was moving to Texas." That colloquy continued:

Q   And the children—you believe the children are still with her?

A   Mm-hmm. But they need to be tooken away from her and give them to somebody can take care of 'em.

Q   Is she not taking care of them?

A   Well, they wasn't eating.

Q   The children were hungry?

A   Yeah.

Q   And why did they not have food?

A   'Cause she don't buy 'em none.

Q   Okay. Is that because they didn't have the money to buy food for the children?

A   Oh, yeah, they had the money.

Concerning the night of Douglas' fall down the cellar steps, she said that Douglas had not been drinking, Janis had been, and that the two of them had been arguing. Apparently Janis was upset because Douglas wouldn't skip going to work and take her places.

Q   Dorothy, was Janis seeing another guy?

A   (Nodding in the affirmative.)

Q   You have nodded affirmatively? You've nodded 'yes'?

A   Yep.

Q   Did Doug know about it?

A   (Indicating in the negative.)

Q   That's not what they were arguing about?

A   No.

Q   Did they ever argue about that?

A   Yeah, when he found out.

Q   When did he find out?

A   Right before he died.

Dorothy Price told me that she found Wayne Bynum lying on the basement floor. She had gotten out of bed the following morning to get a glass of water and heard him call for help. She said she opened the cellar door and saw him lying on the floor. He was "a little bit" conscious and asked if she could get somebody to help him up the steps. She said she called to Amanda and asked her to wake Janis. Then, she said, "They got a quilt; put him on it, brought him up the steps." I reminded her that she had told Dick Rice, on tape, that she thought Janis had pushed him down the stairs the night before. I asked her about that and, without hesitation, she said, "I know she did." That led to another colloquy:

Q How do you know that?
A 'Cause she told me she was. She was going to kill him one way or the other.
Q When did she say that?
A When she was sitting there by me on the couch.
Q Was he there when she said that?
A Yeah.
Q Did he say anything?
A No.
Q Was that while they were arguing?
A Yeah.
Q Is that the same day that he fell down the stairs?
A Yeah.

I asked her whether she had heard that Janis had told people that she, Dorothy, had pushed him down the stairs. She answered that her brother-in-law, Jabow Jolly, who lived in Belton, Texas, had told her that Janis was going to "take her to court" for causing Wayne's death. She said that Jabow had told her that Janis said she was going to make damn sure her mother was put away in a prison.

Just before her deposition terminated, we had another discussion, which I considered to be of interest:

Q   Did you know that Janis was in jail in Texas after Douglas died?

A   No.

Q   Did you know that she was wanted in Texas on a fugitive warrant?

A   She's wanted for lots of things, if you want me to tell you that.

Q   Okay. Would you tell me about it?

A   She killed a man.

Q   What man did she kill?

A   A guy she was going with.

Q   Where did that happen?

A   In Texas.

Q   Why did she kill him?

A   'Cause he was a-messin' around with her kids.

Q   And how did he die?

A   She shot him.

Q   With a handgun?

A   Yeah.

Q   Would that have been before she was married?

A   Yeah.

Q   How old would she have been at that time?

A   About 14.

Q   And she had kids at that time?

A   Yeah.

Q   Was she prosecuted?

A   No. Never did go to trial.

Q   Was she charged?

A   No.

Q   Did they arrest her?

A   No.

Q   Did they not know who had done it?

A   No.

Q   Did the police investigate it?

A   Yeah.

Q   Did they talk with you?

A   I wasn't there when it happened.

Q   Did they talk with Janis?

A   They didn't find her neither.

Q   Okay. Do you know the name of the boy?

A   Gee. Peach-somebody, she called him.

Q   Do you know where that was?

A   It was in Temple, Texas. It's close to Belton.

Q   Okay. And Janis would have been about 14 at the time?

A   Yeah.

Q   How do you know that she shot him?

A   'Cause she told me she did.

Q   And he died?

A   (Nodding in the affirmative.)

Q But nobody ever arrested her, or the police didn't come and talk with her?

A No.

Q Did she run away?

A Yeah.

Q Do you know where she ran to?

A She ran and hid a long time. Then she called me, said, "Mama, can I come home?"

Q Did she tell you before she ran that she had killed the boy?

A No.

Q When did she tell you? After she had run?

A After I had moved up here to Ohio with them.

Q She told you at that time that she had killed this boy?

A Yeah.

Q Do you know of other trouble that she was in?

A No.

Q Do you know that she committed a burglary in Texas?

A Hmm-mm.

Q Do you know that she passed bad checks in Urbana?

A Mm-hmm.

Q And was she charged with that to your knowledge?

A No.

The Deposition of Dorothy Price concluded at 3:00 that afternoon, and the Deposition of Linda Jenkins began just five minutes later. She was an attractive woman, not quite 40 years old, pleasant and articulate. She told us that she resided in St. Paris, Ohio; that she was a licensed social worker, and had been continuously employed by Heartland since August of 1989. In response to my questions, she acknowledged that she was acquainted with Dorothy Price, whom she said was admitted to Heartland in October of 1999. Heartland had been alerted by Champaign County Adult Protective Services that Dorothy was living in a tent at Kiser Lake; and that that Agency went out and got her and caused her to be admitted to the local hospital. Shortly thereafter she was discharged from the hospital and admitted to Heartland, principally because her husband, Walter Price, was already there.

According to Ms. Price, in the spring of 1999, Janis brought both of her parents to Ohio from a nursing home in Kansas because she was unhappy with the care they were receiving there. On April 1, she brought Walter to Heartland and kept Dorothy at home. Then, on April 24, she took Walter back to her home where he stayed for some six to eight weeks until he had to be hospitalized. When I asked why he had to be hospitalized, Ms. Price said, "The story he told us was that Janis was stealing his Social Security check and not buying his medication," and that that omission had resulted in his need to be hospitalized; then, she said that when Walter was released from the hospital, he came back to Heartland and remained there until he died in August of 2000.

Because Walter was indigent, the arrangement for his care was that Medicaid would pay a portion of the cost and that Janis would receive, and turn over to Heartland, his monthly Social Security payments—but she never actually did so. Ms. Price said that at one time Heartland's business office manager had telephoned Shepard Grain Company, where she was employed, in an effort to reach Janis to talk about her failure to turn over Walter's Social Security moneys, but was told that, "Janis had taken off for Kansas because her father had died."

I asked, "Was that a time when her father was alive here?" To which she answered, "Yes."

I asked about the first occasion when she saw Janis after her husband died and whether they'd had a conversation about it. She said she'd seen Janis within a month, hugged her, expressed condolences and asked what had happened. Janis answered "He had a stroke and fell down the steps and died."

"The more we learn about Janis Bynum, the more I'm inclined to believe that she may actually have 'ball-batted' her husband," commented Dick Rice after the depositions had been concluded and we were making the 30-odd mile trip back to Troy. "Maybe not with an actual ball bat, but it's beginning to appear from what we've been hearing that she may well have smacked him from behind with some sort of object—or weapon—hard enough to knock him down the stairs."

"Ball-batted or tire-ironed, or whatever," I remarked. "If, in fact, that's what actually happened, she must have really swung for the fences. From what we see in the medical records, it may well have been the wound to the back of the head that caused his death, rather than the fall down the steps. Remember, the only mark on him was that single wound; he didn't break his neck—or anything else—and if he had been hit from behind, I'd have expected him to have fallen forward and sustained frontal injuries."

Dick chortled at that. "'Swung for the fences,' you say. I've never laid eyes on this gal, but I had the impression that she wasn't a home-run hitter. I haven't heard that she was especially robust, but if that's really what did the job, she sure Lord knocked him out of the park."

"I had the same picture of her as you did and wouldn't have expected her to have that kind of power," I agreed. "And whether or not she did, it certainly sounds like she was mean enough to get the job done."

"Amen to that," said Dick. And that led to a full reprise of what we had been hearing from all the 'witnesses' we'd interviewed thus far.

"However," I cautioned. "We're just speculating—maybe even fantasizing—on the basis of what we've heard so far. For all we know, Doug Bynum may have tripped and fallen down the stairs all by himself—or, he might have gotten all drunked-up and simply took a header, without any participation from anybody. As far as we know, it's unlikely that anyone's going to come forward and tell us that they actually saw what happened. I doubt that we can ever prove what actually happened."

"Agreed," Dick acknowledged.

"On the other hand," I reminded. "We don't have to prove anything. The burden of proof is clearly on the Plaintiff to show that the 'dangerous and defective' condition of the stairway was the direct and proximate cause of Doug Bynum's death—and I don't think they can do that. You and I have seen those steps; they're not just 'stable,' they're rock solid. And the Plaintiff is not going to get an instruction from the Court to the effect that the Dickey's were required by any applicable building code to have installed a handrail to a stairway that's doubtless older than either of us.

"What's still more to the point is the fact that we have every right to argue that Doug Bynum didn't just happen to fall down the steps because they were 'dangerously defective'; we're certainly entitled to produce evidence tending to show that some other factor produced his fall and subsequent death."

"Understood," Dick appended.

"And," I added, "we're just getting started on that line; we still have other fish to fry before we're anywhere close to being ready for trial."

"Speaking of which," Dick interposed. "Remind me again when trial is scheduled; I've got it on my calendar, but don't remember the exact date."

"Trial is scheduled for five days, to a jury, beginning October 16, next year." I answered. "But the more immediate date is the summary judgment date which is September 7. I think this whole thing will go away on summary judgment and that it'll never go to trial."

"Because?"

"Because I don't see any way Mr. Daly can make a *prima facie* case of liability against the Dickeys, and if he can't clear that hurdle, it's over. Let's face it; so far as we now know, he has no evidence whatever to support any of his client's claims, and I fully expect the Judge to dismiss his Complaint.

"However," I continued, "I'm not prepared for us to sit on our hands and hope that happens. We still have a lot of people to talk with—as you well know."

Then, in early December, I received a letter from Mr. Daly, acknowledging the receipt of the Written Interrogatories and Request for Production of Documents which I had served in early November, but confessing that he was unable to locate his client in time to submit the same to her for response. However, he did assure me that "she does check in" with him periodically, and he requested a 20-day extension of the due date for compliance. In the alternative, he expressed an interest in "discussing a proposed settlement for the minor children only along structure terms or whatever additional you might request, and in consideration, we would dismiss this matter and close the case, with respect to all Plaintiffs."

I responded to his request by telephone on December 11 and told him that if he would provide me with the addresses and telephone numbers of the Bynum children, I would consent to the requested 20-day extension. He agreed to do so promptly, and we also agreed that I might schedule the taking of their depositions for a date in February upon the provision of proper notice and without reference to his calendar. I did tell him that I could not respond to his proposal for settlement for the very good reason that such a settlement would be both legally inappropriate and totally unacceptable to the Court. The following day I confirmed our agreement by letter, and directly thereafter he provided the addresses of the children.

And, as might be imagined, as soon as I received the requested information, I arranged for the three children to be subpoenaed for depositions to be held on February 13, 2001, i.e. we would do Erica and Holly, beginning at 9:00 a.m. at the Lampasas County Courthouse in Texas, and then Amanda, beginning at 11:00 a.m. at the nearby Burnett County Courthouse, also in Texas. I filed a formal Notice thereof with the Court, with a copy to Mr. Daly, on December 22, 2000.

In the context of the subpoenas served upon the three children, I was contacted by a Tina Weller, a regional attorney for the Texas Department of Protective and Regulatory Services, who advised that all three girls were currently in foster care in three separate locations.

She suggested that it would be more convenient if all three were deposed at the Burnett County Courthouse rather than as scheduled—a suggestion to which I heartily agreed. She assured me that the Department had no objection to the girls being deposed, but she would not permit them to answer questions concerning confidential information pertinent to the Department's suit, which I presumed was an action to terminate all of Janis' parental rights concerning the children.

She even enclosed a full-page list of those kinds of questions which would be objectionable. In essence, I would not be permitted to in-quire as to their current placements, the schools they were attend-

Sheriff's Deputy Steve Lord

ing, the services and assistance currently being provided by the Department, any therapies being administered, etc., etc. It seemed obvious that the Department's interest was to prevent Janis from discovering where the children were living and/or attending school. I assured her that I had absolutely no intention of inquiring as to any of those matters and invited her to attend the depositions. She expressed her thanks and indicated that she would personally deliver the children to the depositions and assist in any way she could.

I was not at all surprised by Ms. Weller's concerns. I was already under the impression that Janis was in jail somewhere in Texas and that the State Department of Child Protection had assumed responsibility for the children's welfare. I was reminded that Dorothy Price had said that "they should be 'tooken away' from her."

Because it had begun to appear that Doug Bynum's death may not have been an accident, I thought to call lead detective Steve Lord at the Miami County Sheriff's office in Troy to inquire whether they had conducted any kind of investigation. As I recall, I telephoned Steve sometime near the end of the year, and was not surprised at his response. He told me that he had a dim recollection that a fellow had fallen down some cellar steps and later died maybe a year or more ago, but there'd been no suggestion that it might not have been an accident.

"From what you've told me, it sounds like this fella fell down the steps in Miami County, but the Christiansburg squad had him care-flighted to Miami Valley Hospital. So while the precipitating event was in our county, the response team was out of Champaign County, and he died in Montgomery County—apparently as a result of a home accident. It's unlikely that any of that would have made much of an impression in our office," he told me. "But let me look into it and see what I can find; I'll get back to you on it."

When a new civil suit is filed in the Miami Common Pleas Court, the Clerk is required by law to cause summons to be served on those parties named as defendants in the suit; that summons directs the defendants to respond to the Complaint within 28 days after receipt of the summons. Then, after all parties named in the Complaint—or in the responsive pleadings of the defendants—have responded to the allegations contained in any and all of such pleadings, the case is said to be at issue, i.e. ready for further proceedings.

Then, within a short time after the case is at issue, the trial judge to whom the case has been randomly assigned customarily issues a letter to each of the counsel who have appeared in the action asking for their respective best estimates of the time necessary to properly prepare for trial, and—upon receipt of such estimates, the Judge then issues a "Scheduling Order" which establishes certain dates—or deadlines— by which times the parties (i.e., their counsel) are required to perform their several responsibilities directed to an ultimate trial on the merits of the case. In the wrongful death action against the Dickeys, Judge Robert J. Lindeman had received timely responses from both Mr. Daly and myself and thereafter filed his Scheduling Order on October 18 of 2000. In its essence, that order provided, *inter alia*, that:

1.   Plaintiff must disclose the names and addresses of any and all "expert witnesses" whom he intended to use at trial on or before December 15, 2000.

2.   Defendants must, in like manner, disclose their proposed expert witnesses on or before April 16, 2001;

3.   The parties must complete all discovery activities (interrogatories, requests for documents, depositions, etc.) on or before September 7, 2001;

4.   The names of witnesses and copies of exhibits to be used at trial must be exchanged on or before September 7, 2001;

5.   Last date for motions for summary judgment is September 7, 2001;

6.   A settlement conference with the Court was scheduled for September 10, 2001 at 10:30 a.m.;

7.   A Final Pre-Trial Conference was scheduled for September 10, 2001 at 10:30 a.m.;

8.   Trial of the action to a jury was scheduled for

Tuesday, October 16, 2001, beginning at 8:45 a.m. for an estimated 5 days.

On December 20, 2000, I received a copy of a Disclosure of Experts from Mr. Daly, in which he formally advised that the Plaintiff expected to call "Law-Science Technology, Inc. and their Investigators and Forensic Scientist and Accident Reconstructionist" of West Milton, Ohio, to testify at trial. On the following day, I wrote to Mr. Daly, acknowledged his Notice, and requested a copy of his expert's report and opinion letter. Sometime thereafter, he telephoned to advise that his expert had neither examined the premises nor prepared a report—and asked if I could make the Dickey premises available for inspection by his expert so that he could form an opinion concerning the condition of the steps. I agreed to do so and he agreed to provide a copy of the report when it was completed.

Because Mr. Daly had failed to properly notify me concerning his proposed expert witness, I could have moved the Court to exclude the testimony, but I declined to do so.

"Is there some reason you didn't object?" asked Dick Rice.

"Umhmm," I replied. "I know that firm, it's Larry DeHus; I've used him myself on a number of occasions. I also know him to be well-qualified, fair and honest. I'm quite sure we'll like his report."

I did, finally, on February 6, receive Janis Bynum's Response to my Interrogatories and Requests for Production of

Documents from Mr. Daly. The responses were totally worthless to us, except possibly for use on deposition—and/or the imposition of sanctions if I were to move the Court for the appropriate orders. Just as an example, my Interrogatory #11 asked:

> *To your knowledge,* had the said Douglas Bynum, Jr. ever asserted or prosecuted a claim for money damages or awards, either informally or formally, against any person, firm, corporation or other entity in any judicial, administrative or other forum?
>
> The answer given was: *Unknown.*

Apart from their being essentially "non-answers" and failures to answer at all, the Response was neither signed by Janis and notarized (as required), nor signed by Mr. Daly, with proof of service on me.

"Now what?" asked Dick Rice when I reported to him concerning the same. "What do you propose to do about it?"

"I'll just stick it in the file for now," I answered readily, "The fact that she's failed utterly to comply with the Rule or to supply meaningful answers will come back to haunt her—both on deposition and at trial. In point of fact, I'm inclined to doubt that she even participated in answering the interrogatories; I'd be willing to bet that Mr. Daly is only rarely in contact with his client and that the reason for the non-answers is that he simply didn't have the requested information available. I think he just went through the motions of supplying what he had and ignoring that which he didn't have."

"Really?" asked Dick. "What makes you think that?"

"Well," I answered. "First off, remember that Janis Bynum didn't sign them—or acknowledge them. Next, consider that we believe her to be in a Texas jail somewhere; we don't know exactly where, and I doubt if Daly does either. Then look at the answer to our Interrogatory No. 2 where we asked her to provide each of the several addresses where she has resided during the 10 year period immediately preceding the filing of her Complaint. Her answer: '5444 East State Route 55, Casstown, Ohio. Will supplement with additional addresses.' Hell, that's the Dickey farm where she lived with her husband before he was killed; we both know she's resided at other addresses both before and after her husband's death. She (or rather Mr. Daly) didn't even provide the address listed on her initial Complaint, which was 1727 Arnold Drive, in Green Bay, Wisconsin.

"I think that answer really means that Mr. Daly will attempt to supplement it when he gets the real answer from his client. And, let's look at some of the other responses:

Interrogatory No. 4 asks her to list, in chronological order the title of each job or position she's held from the time she entered the work force, together with the names of each employer, the dates of each such employment, et cetera. The Answer: 'Farm worker, Self Employed' Here again, we both know she was employed by Shepard Grain Company when her husband died, I'd have thought Daly would have come up with a better answer to that one.

Interrogatory No. 11 asks if she's ever pled or been convicted of any crime or misdemeanor. The Answer: 'Unknown.'

Here again, we both know that she's been convicted of burglary, but it kinda looks like Mr. Daly doesn't.

"Bottom line is—like I said before—Mr. Daly has simply tried to 'wing it' without any of the answers being supplied by his client. When the time comes, we'll feed it back to him."

Along about mid-afternoon on Monday, February 12, I'd swung by Dick Rice's office in Troy, and picked him up for the 20 minute drive to the Dayton International Airport. I had previously—and facetiously—asked him whether he wanted to accompany me to Burnet, Texas, for the depositions of the three Bynum girls, and what I got for an answer was a mock eye-roll and an inquiry of his own, "Is that supposed to be a serious question?"

"Not really," I'd answered. "I assumed you'd want a chance to take a day or two out of your overstuffed office for a field trip."

"My office is a lot more comfortable than yours, Bud," he informed me. "And the coffee is a far, far better brew than that stuff you serve, too. I'm every bit as anxious as you are to eyeball these young girls and hear what they can tell us first-hand."

"That's kinda what I thought when I asked my secretary to make airline reservations for two," I assured him.

It was well after dark by the time we arrived at San Antonio International, gathered our brief cases and our overnights and rented a car for the hundred-odd mile drive to Burnet, Texas. Then, roughly four hours later, we had caught a quick meal en route and found accommodations at a small roadside motel just outside the city limits. I had initially planned to seek out the county courthouse before calling it a night, but when I learned that the town had a total population of some six thousand souls, I felt confident that we'd have no difficulty finding the courthouse in the morning.

We had spent most of our trip time, both on the aircraft and in the rental car, discussing the case in general and speculating about what we might learn from the Bynums' three daughters. I reminded him of the conditions I had agreed to in my communications with the Texas Child Protective people and their agreement to physically present the children at the Burnet Courthouse for the purpose of our examining them. Once they had been satisfied that we were entirely comfortable with their conditions, they could not have been more accommodating.

"Why all the conditions?" Dick asked.

I rehearsed with him my earlier cursory explanation. "It's my understanding Janis Bynum is currently in custody and that the three girls have been taken by the Child Protection people and placed in separate foster homes for the indefinite future, and that the authorities have anticipated that, at whatever time Janis is released, she will try to find them and physically kidnap them—either from the foster homes, the schools they are attending, or even off the streets.

"I'm sure that the Protection people are well aware that these kids were living in tents in Ohio—and probably in Texas as well—and so far as we know, they haven't been in school since their father died and Janis has apparently moved them from Ohio to Florida, then to Ohio, and back to Texas, and God only knows where else. I'd also be willing to bet that they haven't been particularly well-cared for either, things like regular meals, medical care, proper hygiene, decent clothing—or even appropriate parental supervision.

"Actually, I'm kind of proud of these Child Protection people; I'm sure the kids are in one helluva lot better situation than when they were with their mother—and whatever boyfriends and other hangers-on she might have been keeping house, apartment, shed, trailer or tent with. I'll be surprised if she ever gets them back—and I think that's a good answer to a bad situation."

"Well," Dick agreed. "This gal, this Janis Bynum, certainly seems to be a bizarre personality—in a lot of respects—beginning, I'd imagine, with her parenting skills, and then running an entire gamut of behavioral abnormalities. Neither of us has laid eyes on her as yet—and probably won't for awhile—but, from all we've heard thus far, she seems to be something less than a paragon of virtue—as a mother, or simply as a person I'd want to associate with."

"How would you rate her as a sociopath?" I interjected. "Or, perhaps even as a potential psychopath?"

"Ask me again after we've finally met her," he hedged.

The following morning, we managed to pull ourselves out of bed early enough to shave, shower, dress and catch a quick breakfast at one of the two local eateries we'd discovered on the way to the courthouse. As anticipated, we had no difficulty locating and identifying that edifice; it dominated the center of town like a Colossus. Neither did we have any difficulty in locating an attractive, efficient-looking young woman who introduced herself as Dana Montgomery, our court reporter. She had driven in from nearby Austin, Texas, that morning. Not only had she arrived long before we did, but had already secured permission for us to use the courtroom for our depositions and had set up her stenographic equipment and arranged a grouping of chairs around one of the counsel tables within the bar. And even though Dick and I had arrived some ten minutes before 9:00, she met us at the courthouse door, introduced herself and escorted us to the courtroom itself.

Upon our entry into the courtroom, we were introduced to a small grouping of five people, all of whom had arrived before we had. Because I had already communicated with Konnetta Cloud and Tina Weller of the Texas Child Protection Agency, their names were familiar to me and their presence was not unexpected. However, I had not expected Wanda Bynum, Roxanne Mancuso, or Ellie Krueger, all of whom I assumed were either the current custodians of the Bynum children or their representatives. I also guessed that Wanda Bynum was the children's paternal grandmother. In any event, no explanation was made as to the reason for the presence of these latter three persons and I felt constrained not to inquire; if their presence had been arranged by the Child Protection people, they were most certainly acceptable to me. The children themselves had already been segregated and would remain so until they were to be produced, one by one, for the depositions. It had been previously arranged that a copy of the stipulation which we had entered into with the Child Protection Agency would preface each of the three depositions.

Because Amanda Bynum was the eldest of the three girls, I opted to call her first. In response to my inquiries, she told me that her name was actually Amanda Lynn Jolly. She had been born prior to Janis' marriage to Douglas Bynum, and he was not her biological father. Nonetheless, she had always been treated as his daughter and had taken his name. She said she had been born 'somewhere in Texas' in 1986 and would be 15 years old on March 15. Without being specific, we agreed that she currently resided in Texas 'within 100 to 150 miles' from Burnet; that she was a freshman in high school and was a very good student, all A's and B's. That came as somewhat of a surprise to me since she had not been in school since before her father's death until after the Ohio Child Protection Agency had intervened in the spring of 2000.

She described for me that which sounded much like a nomadic existence. Without being at all precise with the dates, she first told of living in Florida with her family: Janis, Douglas, and her two sisters; her next recollection was that she and her sister Holly came to St. Paris, Ohio, to live in a camper with their paternal grandparents, Douglas Wayne Bynum, Sr. and Wanda Joyce Bynum, and her uncle and aunt, Dustin and Crystal Bynum. Her younger sister, Erica, had remained in Florida with her parents. Then, after maybe half a school year, Janis, Douglas, and Erica moved to Ohio and the family was reunited in a house in Thackery, Ohio, and her Bynum grandparents moved into a home next door to them. Then, she said her parents 'went and got Grandma and

Grandpa Price from an old folks home,' and the seven of them lived there for perhaps a year until the spring of 1999 when she, her father, mother, sisters and Grandma Price moved into the Dickey rental house; Grandpa Price, she said, had been placed in a nursing home before their last move. Then, she related that, maybe five days after her father's death, Mike Warner had moved in with her mother and the family, and that shortly thereafter, the entire menage had gone to Florida where they lived in tents and a trailer for a week or so, then picked up her uncle, Danny Jolly, somewhere in Georgia, and they all returned to Ohio and took up residence in two tents and a trailer at Kiser Lake until she and her sisters were "captured" by the County Sheriff and placed in foster care for a month or so; and then, finally, some few months after being restored to their mother's care, mother and daughters ultimately moved to Texas, where their mother was arrested and the three girls were again taken into protective custody and placed in foster care—although we didn't discuss that latter circumstance because of my agreement with the Texas authorities.

When I asked her what she remembered about her father's death, she answered: "Everything." And that dialogue continued:

Q   Would you tell me?

A   Well, as the day—the beginning of the day, my mom and dad got in a fight and he hit the window of his car and hurt his hand.

Q   Were they outside the house?

A   Outside.

Q   And they were having a fight?

A   Uh-huh.

Q   Physical fight or just yelling and screaming?

A   Just yelling and screaming.

Q   So they were having a fight outside, and your dad hit the windshield?

A   Uh-huh.

Q   Or window?

A   Windshield.

Q   Open hand, fist?

A   Fist.

Q   Okay. Just in frustration and anger?

A   Uh-huh.

Q   Okay. Go ahead.

A   And then when they all calmed down and stuff and we went back inside, I tried to wrap—wrap my dad's hand together. He was complaining it hurt really bad. It was really swollen. And he started drinking because it takes the pain out of his hand.

Q   What was he drinking?

A   Busch.

Q   Busch beer?

A   Uh-huh.

Q   And—what time of day was this?

A   Afternoon. It was almost night.

Q   What happened next?

A   Well, my grandmother was up listening to the radio with me and my dad.

Q   Was your grandmother wheelchair confined at the time?

A   Yes, but she could walk.

Q She could walk?

A Uh-huh. It was more convenient for her to be in a wheelchair. And then everyone went to bed, my mom, my two sisters, they went to bed. And my dad and I, we just sat there and talked and singed with the radio.

Q Was your grandmother in bed also?

A No, she was still watching us, laughing.

Q So there were the three of you there?

A Yeah. And then me and my dad danced and so—and my grandma, she kept saying, "Well, I'm going to bed. I'm tired." So she went to bed and we just kept on dancing and talking and laughing and stuff. And then I started getting tired, so I told my dad good night and I went up to my bedroom to go to sleep. But when I got up there I wasn't tired, so I just started cleaning up my room. I came downstairs to put trash up and things that I got out of my room. And I could hear him snoring in the bedroom. He was a bad snorer.

Q In the bedroom that he shared with your mother?

A Yes.

Q They stayed in the same bed?

A Uh-huh.

Q Door open?

A Huh-uh. It was shut.

Q And you could hear him snore through the door?

A He was a bad snorer. And I started laughing. It was kinda funny. I went back up to bed and watched *I Love Lucy*; I have a TV in my bedroom. And then while I was getting ready for bed, I went downstairs again to use the restroom and I didn't hear him snore. I thought that was kinda weird, but I didn't think anything about it. I thought he might have went outside or something, because he was basically outside all the time. So I went upstairs and went to sleep. It was turning daylight, like early in the morning. And probably an hour later my baby sister, Erica, she came up there waking me up. She said, "Amanda, come on, Dad's hurt really bad."

Q What time do you think that was?

A It was probably 5, 6 o'clock in the morning.

Q Still dark?

A Yeah, like dawn or something. And I got up and went downstairs. I thought they were just pulling my chain just to get me out of bed. I went to the basement stairs and my dad was laying on his back—he was laying on his back down on the bottom of the stairs. I went down there and my mom was over him trying to get his attention.

Q Your mom was already down there?

A Yeah. So was Holly. She was down there, too. And I went down there and he was like coughing and stuff. And I told my mom, "Mom, you've got to turn him over, he's gonna choke on his own spit." And when we did, this foam came out of his mouth and he was mumbling something. You couldn't understand him. And I told mom to—we had to bring him upstairs to get him off this cold floor. So my mom, she grabbed his head thing, and me and my sister grabbed his legs. We took him upstairs and laid him down and we covered him up. And my mom was trying to feed him coffee and breakfast, because she thought he was just having a hangover or something. And I went outside to mow the grass, because the day before he told me to finish up the job. And then all of a sudden my Aunt Barbara and Melvin came over. They went inside, and then my mom ran out and she said, "I'll be back, watch your sisters, I'm gonna go call 911," and stuff. And the next thing I knew he was getting shipped off in a helicopter.

Q Let me just ask you a couple of things about what you've just told me. When you went to the bottom of the stairs and saw your father lying there on his back, your mother was there, and one or both sisters?

A One. Holly.

Q Where was Erica?

A She was upstairs looking down from the doorway.

Q Was there any blood at the bottom of the stairs?

A No, sir.

Q Could you see any kind of a wound or cut on your father?

A No, he didn't have anything except his hand. His hand was still swollen, but that was all.

Q How long was he down at the bottom of the stairs after you got up?

A Not real long. Probably 20, 30 minutes, and then we brought him up.

Q And the reason you brought him up?

A He was on cement, and it was really cold.

Q Whose idea was it to bring him upstairs. Your mother's?

A No, mine.

Q So you got up around or about 5:00, and I understand that's just your best guess; would he have been carried upstairs by about 5:30 in the morning?

A Yeah.

Q Did he vomit at all while he was downstairs?

A It was foam and vomit and whatever else, and stuff, mixed. I don't know.

Q Okay, so let's assume he's upstairs, on the floor, at 5:30 or thereabouts in the morning. When did your mother go to call 911?

A I don't know when she—probably an hour or two, maybe three—

Q Some reason she waited that long?

A She didn't know nothing was wrong with him. She thought he had a hangover or something from the beer he drank that last night or stuff like that.

Q Awhile ago you mentioned your aunt and uncle; who is that again?

A My aunt Barbara Bynum and my uncle Melvin Bynum. They live in St. Paris.

Q How did they happen to be on the scene that morning?

A They were just coming over to visit.

Q Do you remember when they arrived?

A I—I'm not sure.

Q Did they get there before the emergency squad?

A Yeah. When they got there—when they went inside and for just a little bit, like 20 minutes, then my mom came outside saying, "I'm going to go call 911. Watch your sisters," and things like that.

Q When your aunt and uncle arrived and saw your father lying on the floor, did they say anything about his condition that you heard?

A   I was outside mowing the grass.

Q   Did you visit your father in the hospital?

A   Only once. It was on the day he died.

Q   Did your father ever say anything to you about what had happened to him?

A   No. On the morning we found him, he only said his hand hurt—the one he'd hit the windshield with the day before—and that he didn't want any coffee or anything. Then when I saw him in the hospital, he was unconscious.

Q   Did your mom ever tell you what happened to your father?

A   No, she didn't. All she said, that the doctors said he was bleeding on both sides of his brain.

Q   Did you ever see a wound or injury?

A   No.

Q   Did you ever hear your mother suggest that your father had had a stroke and fallen down the stairs?

A   No.

Q   Did you ever hear your mother say that your grandmother had pushed him down the stairs?

A   Yeah. One time she said that to me, and I didn't believe her.

Q   Did she say that she'd seen that happen?

A   No. She told me that she just thought she might have.

In response to my further questioning Amanda confirmed her mother's relationship with Mike Warner, that he'd lived with her for a considerable period of time, that then Mike Warner and the whole family had journeyed to Florida to pick up her uncle Danny, finally found him in Georgia, she said, and then the whole group had returned to Ohio and set up housekeeping in two tents, one large and one small, and two trucks and her father's car at a campground at Kiser Lake. She said that she and her sisters ate whatever her mother and Mike Warner brought them, that none of them had been in school since the spring of 1999, and they lived at Kiser Lake until they were "captured" and placed in foster care; all of it pretty much what we'd already learned from other sources. Then, she said, after several months, or so, their mother was released from custody and rented an apartment in Terre Haute, along with Mike Warner, and the children were returned to her and placed in school in St. Paris where they finished the school year. She told me that within a short time later— and before school was out—Mike Warner split and Janis and the girls moved again, this time to cohabit with a man named Timothy Stapleton in his nearby home. Their next change of circumstance occurred after school was out for the summer. It seems that Janis then split with Timothy Stapleton and moved herself and the girls back to Texas. And finally, shortly after they had arrived in Texas, Janis was arrested, and the girls were taken into protective custody. When I asked her how long her mother was detained in custody, she said, "I don't know. They have all the answers," and pointed to the Child Protection representatives.

Then, when I revisited the relationship between her parents, the dialogue proceeded along the following lines:

Q How did your mother and father get along; did they fight a lot?
A Yeah, they fought a lot.

Q   And when they fought, did they scream and yell at each other?

A   Yes, sir.

Q   Did you ever see either one of them strike the other one?

A   Yes, sir.

Q   Who struck whom?

A   Basically my mom always hits my dad and stuff like that, but one time or two my dad got tired of her yelling at him and hitting him all the time, and he just let her have it. I started laughing.

Q   That was okay? When he let her have it, was that with an open hand, closed fist, or—

A   Open hand. One time it was a closed fist, but what I was laughing at was open hand, because I thought she deserved it.

Q   Did it knock her down?

A   No. It kinda surprised her, but—

Q   When your mother would strike him, what did she use; her hand?

A   Her hand, her fist, kick him a little. She was a little midget. She couldn't do much.

Q   She was what?

A   A midget. She was only five foot.

Q   Did she ever use anything to hit him with?

A   She used to throw things at him.

Q   Like what?

A   If there was a book laying around, throw that. If there was a clothes hanger, pillows, shoes,—you name it, she'd throw it.

Q   How many times do you suppose you saw your father or mother hit one another?

A   Often.

Q   On a weekly basis?

A   More like every other day or something like that.

Finally, just before I let her go, I asked Amanda if she'd be good enough to sketch the interior layout of the Dickey house and label the various rooms on each of the upper two floors and to indicate the location of the stairway leading to the basement. She was good enough to do so and we marked her two sketches as Exhibits 1 and 2. That led to a short dialogue in order that I might better understand her sketch, the location of the various rooms we had discussed, the stairway itself, who slept where, and a myriad other items too numerous to mention.

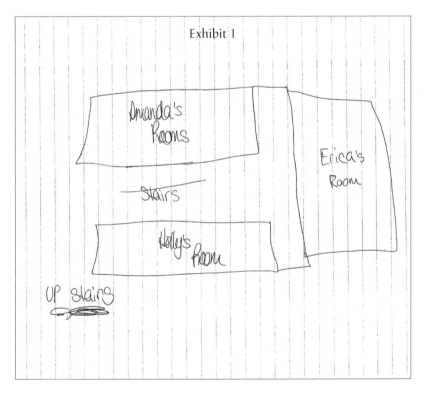

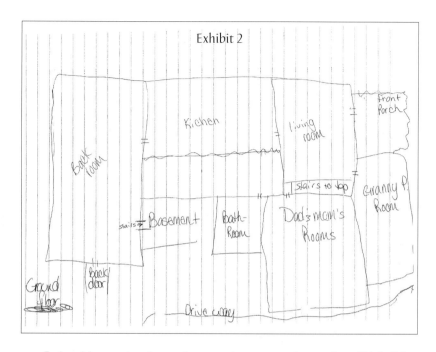

Exhibit 2

I should mention here that on those occasions when Dick Rice attended our depositions, it had always been my custom to provide him with a legal pad and a pen so that he could write me notes to suggest a question or a line of questions he'd like me to put to the witness. That practice had served me well, because Dick always had a good handle on the facts of our cases and because he frequently thought of something I had missed. And because of the complexities involved in this particular fact pattern, he had already written me quite a number of such notes to the point that on one occasion I facetiously threatened to take his pen away from him.

Then, when I began to ask Amanda concerning the rooms on the second floor room, Dick wrote me yet another note, and I interrupted my question to engage in a short colloquy with Dick, which the Court Reporter dutifully transcribed:

MR. FULKER: Oh, I thought we had taken your pen away and you wouldn't write me any more questions.

MR. RICE: I have another pen.

After which we took a short recess.

Amanda's deposition had lasted about two hours. There was no cross-examination because neither Mr. Daly, nor any other representative of Janis Bynum, had appeared to cross-examine. We next proceeded with the depositions of Erica, who would be 12 in April, and Holly, who would be 14 in August. Their testimony was almost entirely consistent with Amanda's, and for that reason neither of them took nearly as much time as did Amanda's.

However, we did have an interesting discussion near the end of Holly's deposition:

Q Did you ever hear your mother tell anybody that she believed your father had had a stroke and fallen down the steps?

A Huh-uh.

Q Did you ever hear anybody suggest that your mother had pushed him down the stairs?

A Uh-huh.

Q Who suggested that?

A My whole family.

Q Okay. Who would that include?

A My aunts—it's all on my dad's side.

Q Would that include the aunt that was over there that morning?

A Yeah.

Q She suggested that maybe your mother pushed him down the steps?

A Yeah.

Q Did she say that to your mother?

A No.

Q She said that to you?

A (Nods head)

Q Who else in your family suggested that your mother pushed him?

A My grandparents, my—

Q Grandparents, Bynum?

A Yeah.

Q They both suggested that?

A Yeah. And just everybody. My aunt—my aunts—his—I never heard his brother say it, but my great aunt and my great uncle.

Q Anybody else?

A His friends. Leroy.

Q His friends suggested that, also?

A Leroy Spenser, his best friend.

Q What do you think happened?

A I don't know. I—when I first—when everything happened, you know, I thought my dad was drunk and fell down the steps. But when I stopped—when I came down here I stopped—and everybody was talking about it and I stopped and looked back at what happened, and it did kind of does look like my mom did it, but—

Q Okay. What do you think happened?

A   It kind of looks like my mom did push him down the stairs, and my grandma. Because my grandma kept saying he was up dancing with her until 12 o'clock, which I was there when he went to bed. He was not dancing with anyone.

Much to my surprise, we had managed to finish with the three girls, and to express our thanks to the Texas Child Protection Agents for their assistance and co-operation, in time to catch a quick lunch before we began our four-hour drive back to the San Antonio International Airport in time for our flight back to Dayton. We stopped at the same small, but extremely hospitable diner where we'd had breakfast that morning. I don't actually remember what Dick had for lunch, but I clearly remember that I had that which I considered to be the best grilled cheese sandwich I'd ever eaten—or perhaps it only seemed so because I was intensely satisfied with both the course and content of the depositions we'd just finished.

In any case, the luncheon break provided both the opportunity and a congenial climate to begin our ruminations concerning the case as we had apprehended it to be, fully augmented by what we'd learned from the girls. Dick began with the anticipated questions. "Well, John, what'd you make of all that? Was it worth the trip?"

"Oh, yes," I replied. "I think it was definitely worth the trip—for a great number of reasons."

"Agreed," said Dick. "Let's talk about it."

"Well," I began. "The first thing that impressed me was the very obvious maturity of each of the three young girls and the equally obvious candor and forthrightness with which they responded to my inquiries. Consider for a moment their childhood experiences—just those that we've learned about—their personal and family histories, their collective exposure to their mother's apparently ungovernable temper, her physical assaults on their father and her openly sluttish behavior, their own nomadic lifestyle, moving from place to place like chess pieces, living in tents, cars, and a truck in a public park in the middle of an Ohio winter, kept out of school for months, their having been poorly cared for, often hungry, ultimately "captured" by the authorities and placed in foster homes, first in Ohio and again in Texas—considering all that, I would never have expected them to be as amiable, seemingly bright, candid and articulate as we found them to be."

"Me, too," Dick agreed. "All three of them seemed like decent kids. If we didn't know better, we'd probably have figured them to have been the products of an above average, middle-class American home, well cared for and properly instructed. I was as surprised—and every bit as impressed as you were. I liked them—and I'm glad they're in state-approved foster homes. I hope they stay there."

"I'd guess that they will," I responded. "If the Texas Protective Agency has taken such great pains to isolate them from their mother, I would certainly imagine that their current placements are intended to be permanent."

We had continued our discussion, both of the children themselves and their testimonies throughout our trip back to the airport and then during the flight back to Dayton. I think we were in agreement that their respective responses and accounts were essentially consistent, one with another, and confirmed much of what we had already heard from other witnesses.

"I'm sure that you noted that Janis had apparently refused to call for an ambulance or an EMT squad until Uncle Mel and Aunt Barbara arrived on the scene, and that within some 20 minutes after their arrival, she rushed over to the Dickey home to call for assistance. That would seem to suggest that she was hoping he'd die at home—and without receiving any medical attention. And, I'm guessing that Uncle Mel and Aunt Barbara insisted she make the call, and, of course she had no realistic choice other than to summon help."

"That kinda confirms what I'd suspected all along," said Dick. "I would imagine, though, that if he didn't die within a short time, she'd have felt constrained to call for help, but I think you're right. She was gonna wait as long as she thought she could."

Later on in our conversation, I remarked, "I was also intrigued to learn from Holly that quite a number of people—her whole family, she said—believed that Janis had pushed her husband down the stairs…"

"Her whole family on the Bynum side," Dick interrupted.

"True enough, that's what she said. But who is there on Janis' side to disagree with that accusation?" I answered. "Remember, Janis' mother has said the same thing on deposition. And, remember that Holly also said that a lot of her friends were of the same opinion."

"As did some of the sheriff's deputies, according to Mike Warner."

"And," I added. "You'll remember Holly's answer when I asked her what she thought had happened. I made a special note of it. I've got it right here; she said, 'It kind of looks like my mom did push him down the stairs…' As a practical matter, that seems pretty damning."

"But is any of that admissible in court? Don't you fellas have what they call a hearsay rule? Doesn't that preclude introduction of that kind of 'everybody thinks so' evidence?" Dick asked the obvious questions.

"Yeah, we do have such a rule, and yeah, it does prevent us from using that kind of 'he said or he thinks' evidence." I conceded. "But, if we ultimately go to trial, we may find a way to slip it in anyway."

"Like how?" Dick wanted to know.

"There are ways," I replied. "As a rule, hearsay evidence usually has to be objected to in order to require exclusion; sometimes the judge himself will exclude it himself without objection, but not always. And, keep in mind, since Mr. Daly was not in attendance at the depositions, he has certainly failed to object to it on the record. I recognize that he can still object to it prior to the transcript being read at trial, but that will be difficult for him to do if he hasn't seen the transcript—and we both know that he has neither attended, nor ordered a copy of the transcript, of any of the depositions we've taken thus far.

"Besides which," I appended, "There are other uses of deposition transcripts besides their introduction at trial. For example, they can be used in support of a Motion for Summary Judgment, which I most certainly intend to ask for. In that event, the Judge will read the transcript and will, at least, become aware of what the rest of the world 'believes' to have happened."

"Tricky," Dick said. "But is that ethical?"

"Perfectly," I responded. "Here again, I remind you that the burden of proving a case against the Dickeys is on the Plaintiff. It's not our job to prove what happened. All we need to do is show that there is a distinct and reasonably credible alternative to Plaintiff's theory of recovery. I'm very much elated to learn that there is a reasonable and widespread belief that he didn't fall down those steps because of any defect in the stairway."

At another point in our general discussion of the case—and of our antagonist, Janis Bynum—I remarked that, "You know, this gal must be a real piece of work."

"How's that?" Dick asked.

"Well, let's take a look at her," I mused aloud. "If her mother is to be believed, she shot and killed her boyfriend at age 14 and fled; she apparently had Amanda, either in or out of wedlock, at what must have been a very early age; she pled guilty to a felony and burglary, in Texas, then violated her probation, fled Texas to avoid re-arrest, ended up in Ohio and married Doug Bynum, and allegedly cheated on him, and fought with him on an every other day basis, perhaps killed him, then, within a matter of days or weeks at the most, she entered into a sexual relationship with Mike Warner, who has said that she threatened him twice with a knife, moved her entire menage to a campground at Kiser Lake where they lived in tents and motor vehicles, had her children taken from her by the sheriff's department, broke up with Mike Warner and moved in with a Timothy Stapleton for a short spell before she moved back to Texas, got herself arrested for some reason and her children taken from her by the Texas Child Protection Agency. Add to that, from what we've been told, she moved her parents to Ohio and stole their social security checks.

"I think that history, if believed, fairly describes 'a real piece of work,'" I concluded.

"Can't argue that," agreed Dick.

"Neither of us has ever met or even laid eyes on this gal, but she must have something going for her," I added. "From what we've heard, it seems as though she has a ferocious temper, a criminal record and a disgraceful set of values, but she apparently doesn't have any difficulty attracting men. Sounds to me as though she changes paramours as casually as you and I change shirts.

"I keep wondering what it is we're dealing with here."

"Maybe she's just an exceptionally charming free spirit," Dick offered.

"Or maybe just some kind of sex-bomb," I muttered tightly.

"Sounds to me like she was sufficiently explosive to have been some kind of bomb—sex or otherwise," said Dick.

"Or maybe both?" was my wry response.

By the time we had deplaned in Dayton and driven home, I think we'd both had enough of the case of The Estate of Douglas Bynum vs. Dickey to last us for a while.

Early on in his investigation, Dick Rice had somehow learned that after her husband's death, Janis Bynum had developed a suspicious-looking relationship with a 16-year-old boy who resided in nearby Christiansburg. Dick was sufficiently intrigued by that information that he made further inquiries and found that his name was Brian Lansing and that he had spent a significant amount of time at her residence, including several overnight stays.

"How the hell did you stumble on that information?" I asked him.

"I found it under a rock," he answered glibly. "Anyway, I thought it might lead us to something helpful, so I went out to his home and took a recorded statement from him."

"I'm hoping you had a parental consent," I remarked.

"Of course I did. His mother not only consented, but actually participated in the procedure," he said. "It's all on tape. You want to see it or not?"

When I nodded affirmatively, he reached into his brief case and extracted an 8-page transcript of his interview with Brian Lansing and with his mother, Debbie Lansing. It was dated August 30, 2000 and certainly made interesting reading. Brian said he had said that he resided in Christiansburg, Ohio, was 16 years old, and a 9th grade student at the local high school. He said he'd first met Janis Bynum "about a year ago" at Mike Warner's store, where he occasionally helped out. He said that he and Janis became close friends, went camping together, and that he "stayed out there for a little while and helped them out." In response to Dick's questioning, he provided a minutely accurate description of the Dickey house where Janis was living. Then, their dialogue continued:

DR Okay, Janis' husband, Douglas was involved in an accident, did Janis ever talk to you about that accident?

BL   Yes, all the time.

DR   What did she tell you about it?

BL   She told me that during one of the nights her mother and her husband was not getting along and they were getting into an argument and as he was coming down the steps she tripped him and pushed him at the same time. He fell down the steps.

DR   Which steps were they?

BL   The ones going to the basement.

DR   OK, he was going down the steps and the mother pushed him, tripped him, pushed him down the steps.

BL   Yes.

DR   Did Janis know any of this happened?

BL   She told me that she didn't know what happened until she came out and saw the mother sitting at the top of the steps looking down.

DR   OK, this is right after it happened that she saw it?

BL   Yes, she heard something fall and she went looking to see what it was.

DR   Did Janis say that this was in the daytime, nighttime?

BL   She said it was about 11 or 12 at night.

DR   Did she say what she did then after she realized what had happened?

BL   I didn't know anything about that, that's all she said.

DR   Now, her mother, you said was sitting at the top of the steps?

BL   In a wheel chair, yes.

DR   OK, so she was a lady in a wheel chair?

BL   Yes.

Further along in Brian's statement, there was a reference to Mike Warner; that discussion was quite brief:

DR What happened with Mike, did she ever say?

BL Yeah, Mike ticked her off and she hit him upside the head with a tire iron.

DR Where at?

BL I'm not sure.

DR So she told you that she got mad at him and hit him upside the head with a tire iron?

BL Yes.

And, near the very end of the transcript, we find:

DR Debbie, do you have anything to add to this?

DL Yes. Janis came to my house one time only, when Brian cut his relationship with them. He was staying with his father up the street. When he came back to live with me she came to the house one day and when she came in she hugged Brian, patted his knee, sat down and told me, in front of Brian, that everyone thought she killed her husband, but she didn't; that her mother had done it. She told me the same story that Brian said about her mother being crazy and she had caused trouble before and so they had taken her away.

"Hey, Dick, good job," I enthused. "It doesn't really matter whether Janis did it or grandma did it, there's no way Daly can prove a case of liability against the Dickeys; no one has yet suggested that either of *them* tripped or pushed him down the stairs. How about my arranging the deposition of both Brian and his mother?"

"Sounds good to me," he answered.

"I'll set it up, give notice to Daly, and we'll take them both under oath."

I had no difficulty getting service on Debbie Lansing, but had still been unable to locate her son. His deposition would have to wait. In the meanwhile we did take Debbie's deposition on February 21, just 8 days after we'd returned from Texas. We didn't elicit a great deal more information from her than we already had from the statement Dick had taken earlier, but there were several nuances worth mentioning. Among other things, we had talked with Debbie about Brian's relationship with Janis:

Q   Beyond just knowing one another, did that acquaintance develop into something more than just a casual acquaintance?

A   Brian started going out to her house quite a bit. He went camping with them a number of times. He stayed the night at her house. I wasn't really pleased with the relationship, but there wasn't anything I could do about it.

Q   Do you know what it was that attracted Brian to that household?

A   He said she was nice to him and she said he helped her do chores. And, you know, with him—well, his father is an alcoholic and so Brian has had some strange relationships. I feel, due to that. I think she befriended him. Maybe she felt sorry for him. I don't know for sure.

Q Do you know whether there was anything sexual between Brian and Janis Bynum?

A I asked him that. I asked him that on two different occasions. In fact, Mr. Rice was there one day when I asked him. And he said, no, there was nothing like that. All I know is when she came to my house the one time, she sat beside him very close on the couch and like had her arm around him and I did not like that.

Q So you have had at least some suspicion that maybe there was something sexual there?

A I just felt very uncomfortable with the whole relationship.

And, at another juncture in her deposition we had the following colloquy:

Q Did you ever have a conversation just with Brian about Doug Bynum's death?

A Yes.

Q Were there more than one of those conversations between you and Brian?

A Yes. There were a couple different conversations and he seemed to feel that she kind of changed the story maybe from one time to the next when she talked to him about the death.

Q Was it your impression she told him more than one story, gave him more than one account?

A Yes.

Q Do you know what those several accounts were?

A I think one time she said something about everybody thought she pushed him down the stairs but she didn't. She said her mother had. The second time, I can't remember if he said that they thought he accidentally fell, but when she came to my home the one time, she looked directly at me and said she did not kill her husband, that her mother did.

Q What was it that caused her to come to your home?

A She was back in town and she missed Brian and she wanted to see him. And so she sat down on the couch close beside him and she told me what a good kid he was and different things like that. And then I think she knew I didn't like her there because she said, "You think I killed my husband, don't you?" I said, "I don't know—I don't know if—what happened. I don't know you people." And she said, "Well, I didn't kill him, my mother pushed him down the stairs." And then she told me her mother was crazy and that's why her and Mike Warner had taken her to Florida and left her mother in Florida and then came back.

Q Did she say they left her mother in Florida?

A Yes.

"Do you remember the old line—or maybe it was a game— about 'Who killed Cock Robin?'" asked Dick after we'd finished Debbie Lansing's deposition. "We seem to be playing that same game with these various versions we're hearing."

"Damned if we're not," I rejoined. "Let's see, thus far we have Janis suing the Dickeys because her husband fell down the rickety stair steps in their old rental property because of the absence of a handrail; now we hear that Janis' wheel chair-confined mother tripped or pushed him down the steps; then we hear from the kids that all the family members on Doug Bynum's side believe that Janis pushed him down the steps—and that her daughter 'kinda' thinks so too; next we hear that Janis told still others that her husband had had a stroke—presumably as he was either climbing up or descending down the steps."

"Kinda makes you wonder what else is out there, doesn't it?" commented Dick.

"One thing about it is, if somebody actually killed our Cock Robin—or even if he had had a stroke, the Dickeys are off the hook," I said. "That is, of course, unless one of the Dickeys pushed him down the steps—and that's one of the things nobody has mentioned as a possibility."

"One of these days, somebody will probably suggest that too," Dick chuckled. "We're not finished yet."

"Hmph," I grunted. "All things are possible. However, we're not yet aware of any evidence—or even a speculation—from anyone other than Mr. Daly, that he fell to his death by reason of a defective stairway or the absence of a handrail. And, of course, Mr. Daly's naked assertion is not evidence."

"True enough," agreed Dick. "And, yes, I did notice that Mr. Daly did not attend this latest deposition either."

"As I had expected," I added.

"By the way," Dick inquired. "How soon do you expect we can take Brian Lansing's deposition."

"Not sure," I responded. "As you know, we've not gotten service on him yet. And, I'm not sure there's any urgency about it. Debbie Lansing's testimony gives us someone who actually heard Janis say that her mother pushed Doug down the steps. That single, direct statement, all by itself, should be sufficient to assure us a non-suit on a motion for summary judgement.

"So, for that reason, I'm not really in a great hurry to depose Brian; we can do that when we get closer to summary judgment or trial."

On the same day, February 21, I wrote to Mr. Daly to confirm our telephone conversation of the day before, in which we had agreed that I might take the depositions of "nominal Plaintiff, Jeffrey D. Livingston (the Administrator of Douglas Bynum's Estate), Plaintiff Janis Bynum and Plaintiffs' designated "expert witness," Larry Dehus; all of those depositions would be taken as on cross-examination, because all of them could be considered as potentially adverse to our side of the case. I also enclosed file-stamped copies of my formal Notices of Deposition for all three.

Less than two weeks later, on March 6, I fielded a call from Plaintiff's designated "Expert Witness," Larry Dehus, and after the customary exchange of pleasantries, he reminded me that I had agreed to make the Dickey rental house available to him in order

John Fulker

that he might examine the same, particularly with reference to the cellar stairway. I acknowledged that I had promised to do so and asked when he would like to do it.

"I don't know, John," he replied. "Whatever suits your convenience. I'd like to do it soon if possible; as you know, I've received your Notice and that tells me I'm under some kind of deadline."

"Yeah, and I'm sorry about that. I can't do it tomorrow, but I do have time the next day, that would be Thursday, the 8th. Will that work for you?"

"Absolutely," he answered. "I can be in your office at whatever time you say and we can drive out to the tenant house together."

"Is 4:45 too late?" I asked. "I've got appointments most of the day, but can easily be finished by then."

"Works for me," he answered. "I'll see you then."

By the sheerest of coincidences, it just happened that my last appointment before the agreed-upon time for Larry and I to visit the Dickey place, was with Gary Nasal, the Miami County Prosecuting Attorney. My prior discussions with Sheriff's Deputy Steve Lord, the deposition transcripts I had supplied him with on a continuing basis, coupled with his own inquiries, had led the two of us to the conclusion that I should make contact with the Prosecutor and advise him of what we had learned thus far.

I spent some time with Gary discussing that which we had learned and what we suspected might have occurred. He agreed that the matter should be closely scrutinized. Ultimately we agreed that once we had taken Janis' deposition, the sheriff's deputies should become involved. They wanted to talk with her, but we had no knowledge concerning her current whereabouts. I told him that I would keep Deputy Lord posted concerning the time and place of the taking of her deposition and suggested that he might arrange to have someone on hand to take her back to the sheriff's office to interview her.

The following day, I called Deputy Lord and he agreed with the plan (I think the idea may have actually originated with him), and I advised him concerning the time we had scheduled for Janis Bynum's deposition. He agreed to have a deputy arrive at my office after the deposition had begun in our downstairs conference room, wait however long her deposition lasted, and then escort her back to the Sheriff's office for their own examination.

When I informed Dick Rice about the arrangement, he rubbed his hands with glee. "Great idea," he enthused. "But what if she doesn't show? We think she's somewhere in Texas, but have no information as to exactly where."

"I know that," I said. "And I don't think Daly really knows where she is either; I suspect that he has nothing more than her telephone number. The fact that he has agreed to produce her for deposition suggests that he is able to confer with her one way or another."

"You're satisfied she'll show?"

"I'd bet on it," I told him. "She's in zugzwang."

"She's where?" he asked. "I thought you said she was in Texas. Is this Zug-whatever located somewhere in Texas?"

"No, no," I laughed. "Zugzwang isn't a place. It's a predicament."

"Explain that, would you?"

"You're not a chess-player, I can see that," I observed. "Zugzwang is a chess term; it's a German term used to describe a position in a chess game where both sides are equal, but the situation is such that the player who is required to move one of his pieces cannot do so without losing the game."

"Okay," he responded. "So how do you figure she's in that situation?"

"That's easy," I said. "If she doesn't appear for deposition, her claims against the Dickeys will be dismissed by the Court; on the other hand, if she does appear, she has to be deposed and takes the chance of being interviewed by the sheriff's office. It's her move, and she loses either way."

"Gotcha," he replied. "I may have to take up chess just so I can understand all these high-falutin' words you lawyers—and chess-players—use."

As it happened, the times and dates of the three depositions scheduled for March 16, were modified by mutual agreement in order to accommodate the schedules of the deponents. The first such deposition, that of Jeffrey D. Livingston, the Administrator for Doug Bynum's Estate, and therefore the actual plaintiff in the case, took precisely seven minutes, from start to finish. Mr. Livingston was a young attorney who had been in the practice for about two years and had been associated with Mr. Daly for "nine months to a year." He said he had been appointed by the Probate Court of Miami County as Administrator of Doug Bynum's Estate on September 11 of 2000. Beyond that fact—and what he had read from Mr. Daly's initial Complaint—he had no personal knowledge of anything or anybody concerned in the litigation against the Dickeys. At one point:

Q Have you ever had an opportunity to interview Janis Bynum?

A No, I have not.

Q Do you have any statements from Janis Bynum in your file?

A No, I do not.

Q Is it fair then for me to conclude that the information you have concerning Janis Bynum, her marital status, her professional status, the events of the incident which occurred on July 11, 1999, constitutes the only knowledge you have of any of those matters and is hearsay?

A Yes.

And, further on:

Q Now, with reference to the specific incident which is the subject of this lawsuit, do you know at this point in time what evidence will be produced on trial to support the allegations of the complaint?

A No, I do not.

Q Do you know what persons will be called to testify in support of the allegations of the complaint?

A No, I do not.

Q   And if you had any knowledge concerning evidence or witnesses, it would only be by virtue of what somebody has told you?

A   That is correct.

Q   And I think you indicated that you have not had any communication at all with Janis Bynum?

A   That is correct.

Q   Have not talked with her on the phone?

A   No, I have not.

Q   You have not received any correspondence with her?

A   No, I have not.

Mr. Livingston's deposition had begun at 12:12 p.m. and was terminated at 12:19 p.m. It was quite clear that he had no personal knowledge whatsoever concerning any aspect of the case. Both Dick and I had anticipated that to be the case, but neither of us liked surprises, and we wanted to forfend against a surprise from that quarter.

The next deposition, that of Larry Dehus, Plaintiff's expert witness began at 1:30 the same day, as originally scheduled. In response to my questions, he stated his name, residence and business addresses, his educational background and experience, and his occupation as a forensic scientist. Inasmuch as Mr. Daly had formally notified me in December that he intended to utilize Law Science Technology (Larry Dehus) as his expert witness at trial, I was much surprised to learn that he had not contacted either the firm or Mr. Dehus prior to

March 6—the same day that Larry had called me to arrange an examination of the Dickey premises and long after my having arranged to take his deposition.

That circumstance also came as a surprise to Dick Rice, who wrote a quick note to me which read "Is that anything like putting the cart before the horse?" My only response was an affirmative nod in his general direction.

Mr. Dehus testified concerning our March 8 visit to the Dickey tenant house for the purpose of his examination and evaluation of the stairwell and the steps leading to the basement. As a part of his examination, he had taken a number of photographs of the house itself and the cellar stairway and steps. He told me that his son, Ben Dehus, a member of his firm, had done some quick research concerning the building itself. He had reported that it appeared from the township records that in 1976 a zoning inspector had prepared a zoning permit relative to a room that was added to the back of the structure. Then, we had the following dialogue:

Q   Do you have a copy of that here?

A   No. No. I don't.

Q   Did that permit address the subject of this action?

A   I don't believe so.

Q   What else was discovered during that investigation or as a result of that investigation?

A   Ben also reported that Miami County began doing structural inspections, building inspections in 1979 and at that time they were doing CABO codes.

A view of the Dickey's rental property

Another view of the Dickey house

Q And are either of those two facts relevant to this proceeding?

A Well, I think they are, yes.

Q Tell me how that is, first with reference to the addition in 1976. I think you said the building permit?

A Sure.

Q First, to whom was that permit issued?

View of the stairway landing

View from the basement

A   I don't know.

Q   Do you know whether or not Mr. and Mrs. Dickey owned the property at that time?

A   No, I don't.

Q   Go ahead and tell me how that's relevant then.

A   Well, this home is obviously an old farmhouse that's doubtless the original structure, probably in excess of a hundred years old, and the standards that would have applied to the constructions of a stairway at that time would have been considerably different than they would have been for the construction of a stairway in more recent times.

Q   Are you suggesting that under this scenario—building built perhaps a hundred years ago, room added in 1976, the county adopts a code in 1979—are you suggesting that at some later time the owners of this building were under a duty to install a handrail and take whatever steps were necessary to bring these steps into compliance?

A   I think that is probable based on my belief that there was a major renovation done that included the addition and the stairway itself.

Q   Wasn't it your belief that that was done in 1976?

A   That's correct.

Q   And that's before the county went with the CABO code, is it not?

A   That's before the county officially started doing inspections.

Q   Specifically what code applied to this building?

A   Well, I don't know if—that's something I've got to research to get an answer to.

Q   Do you know whether any code actually directly applied to that remodeling or whatever was done in 1976?

A   I believe there would have been, yes.

Q   That wasn't quite my question. Do you know whether any code applied in 1976?

A   Well, the best way I can answer your question is I believe that there was. I'll have to confirm that by further investigation.

Q   As we sit here, you don't know what code applied?

A   No.

That dialogue continued far longer than necessary; the essence of it was that Larry had no knowledge as to what, if any, code might have applied to a remodeling performed in 1976—which, of course was some twenty years before the Dickeys had bought that particular farm and the buildings located thereon. We then turned to another subject, more pertinent to the real issue:

Q Did you have any problem with any aspect of the stairway or stairwell other than the absence of a handrail?

A No. The riser heights, the tread depth, the solidness of the stairwell all seemed fine.

Q They were all appropriate?

A Yes.

Q Well, let's cut to the chase here. The Complaint speaks of "the dangerous and defective condition of the basement stairs which were of such a steep degree, unstable, and contained no handrail and that these stairs were in need of a handrail at a minimum to make them suitable for use." Let's take that apart. First, is it your opinion from your inspection and your research that the stairs which you looked at were dangerous?

A Only in that they lacked a handrail.

Q Were they defective?

A Only in that they lacked a handrail.

Q They weren't dangerous because they were steep?

A No, they were not.

Q Were they dangerous because of their instability?

A No.

Q So if you have any criticism at all with reference to the stairs or the stairwell, it would be the sole criticism that they did not have a handrail?

A That's correct.

And finally:

Q You're not prepared to testify that the proximate cause of the death of Plaintiff's decedent was the absence of a handrail or resulted from the negligence of the Dickeys in that particular, are you?

A Not based on the information I have now, no, 'cause I have no information as to the circumstances of the fall.

After Larry Dehus had closed his file, and the court reporter had packed away her equipment, and both had departed, Dick Rice and I remained in the conference room just long enough to evaluate the witnesses and their testimony. Dick remarked, "I was damn sure Dehus was going to agree that the steps were stable, because I was out there right after we got the Complaint, and I jumped up and down on each of them."

"Pretty solid, right?"

"John, I weigh three hundred pounds and I couldn't make any impression on them at all—not even a squeak," he replied with some heat. "And Daly would have had us believe they were rickety? Not hardly!"

"I know," I agreed, "I tried them, too. They felt like concrete to me; they could have been built last week from the way they looked and felt. And they sure Lord weren't any steeper than the ones in my home or office."

"And," he added, "we know that the Dickeys didn't own the building until the mid '90s, so they would have nothing to do with whatever remodeling was done back in 1976."

"We also know," I appended, "that none of the codes presently in effect require the addition of stair rails unless there's a major alteration of the stairway itself. They're grand-fathered.

"Still more to the point, Plaintiffs can't even show what caused Doug Bynum to fall down the steps in the first place; it could just as easily be that he missed a step, stumbled or tripped."

"Or was ball-batted," Dick answered with an impish grin.

The following Monday, March 19, turned out to be D-Day for Janis Bynum. At Mr. Daly's request, we had agreed to defer her deposition until that morning. She did appear, accompanied by Mr. Daly, shortly before 10 o'clock and both were escorted to our downstairs conference room. Our court reporter, Norma de Roziere, was already there and fully set up and ready to proceed. Dick Rice and I had waited in my office until our receptionist advised that all the players were in attendance. As soon as we learned that Janis and her counsel were there, I telephoned Deputy Steve Lord to notify him that the stage was set and to let him know that we would probably finish with her testimony between 3 and 4 o'clock that afternoon. "Good news," he said. "We'll have someone there along about 3:00; if anything changes, let us know. We're anxious to talk with her."

It seems fair to remark that both Dick and I were stunned by Janis Bynum's personal and physical appearance. We had truly expected her to be something of a femme fatale, a sexual "bombshell," sufficiently attractive to turn heads and to draw the attentions of a vast series of eager males. As it happened, that impression was immediately dispelled. She was both plump and frumpy-looking. We had expected her to be five feet tall from her daughter's testimony, but we had not expected her to be somewhere in excess of a hundred-fifty pounds. Neither had we expected her be attired in clothing that looked like something that might have been badly-used and discarded perhaps forty years earlier. To her credit, she seemed civil enough and answered my questions readily and seemingly without rancor.

Her deposition actually began at 10:32 that morning. Following my lead, she gave her full name as Janis Marie Bynum, her date and place of birth as September 29, 1969, Temple, Texas, and told me that she had resided for the past seven months at 1101 Brazos, Menard, Texas, which was the residence of an elderly lady, a Vina Estep, whom she was taking care of, and that she was currently in training to become a nurse's aide. She gave her prior address as 5873 Coffin Station in Terre Haute, Ohio, where she said she had lived since her husband died on July 13, 1999. She said that those were the only two residences she'd had since her husband's death.

She gave a history of having been raised in Brady, Texas, and then, after her parents divorced, she and her mother moved in with her maternal grandmother in Thorndale, Texas, where she attended school as far as the 7th grade, at which time her mother left to live with "this gentleman" and her grandmother took her out of school and "home-schooled" her until at age 16, when she and Douglas were "common law" married in June of 1986. She said her oldest child, Amanda, was born March 5 of that same year. She told me that Amanda was six months old when she and Douglas Bynum had entered into their "common law" marriage. I didn't see fit to question her math.

In response to my next questions, she said that Amanda was not Doug Bynum's daughter, but that of a man named Darwin T. Ludlow who was living in Green Bay, Wisconsin. She and Douglas had assumed the full care and custody of Amanda since she was born— "until recently," she added. She confirmed that she had given birth to three children, Amanda, who had just turned 15, Erica, aged 13 and Holly, aged 11. She added that she had subsequently had a miscarriage, and had had her tubes tied at Fort Walton Beach, Florida, where the family lived until 1993, when they moved to Thackery, Ohio, because Doug's mother had become ill. In Thackery, they shared a two-bedroom trailer with Doug's mother, father, brother and sister—9 persons in all—for some three months until they and their children finally moved into a small apartment next door for another four months, and ultimately into the Dickey house—right after Christmas, or maybe in February, she said.

All of the foregoing was simply by way of background. When we finally got them to the Dickey house, I asked her to sketch the interior layout of their new home, and asked about their family menage, their pets, chickens, domestic animals, and to provide a description of the exterior grounds surrounding the house, all of which she attempted to do. She also described their several employments while living there, odd jobs and, for the most part, she said that both she and her husband worked for the Shephard Grain Company in Fletcher and in Thackery, Ohio.

Ultimately, of course, we got to the day in question. Her description of the events that had occurred on that Saturday afternoon and evening differed significantly from what we had been led to believe. She said that she had left work early that day because she had a tummy ache, got home about 2 o'clock and found her husband and her daughter, Erica, outside working on his truck. She said she'd gone into the house to cook lunch for her mother and the children. Her husband, Wayne, she called him, said he wasn't hungry and Erica remained outside with her daddy. They kept working on the truck through the evening, and when neither would come in for dinner, she made sandwiches and took them outside for them to eat. Finally, at about 10:30, she came out and insisted that they stop; it was too late for Erica to be out.

Moments later, she told me that Erica had come in and gone to bed at 9:45 and that the other two girls were already in bed, and that Wayne came in about 10:00, 10:30:

Q   What did he do when he finally came in?

A   He sat in the living room and turned the stereo on. And I told him, I said, "Will you please turn the music down?" And he goes, "I'm sorry. I didn't know I had it so loud." I said, "It's not very loud, but I don't want the children to get up or Mom to get up." I said, "I'm going to bed." He said, "You still don't feel good?" I said, "No, my tummy is still hurting." He goes, "Well, in the morning, call and see if you can get a doctor appointment." I kinda laughed and did my finger like this (indicating). I said "What am I supposed to call on?"

Q   You did not have a telephone?

A   No, we did not have a telephone. He goes, "Well, you can go down to the pay phone in Fletcher and use it." He kind of come up and he gave me a hug, and he goes, "I'll turn it down. I promise." And he tucked me into bed. He had this thing about tucking me in bed.

Q   So you went to bed before he did?

A   Yes.

Q   And he tucked you in?

A   Yes.

Q   So what time do you think you went to bed that night?

A   It was about 11:15, because I was cleaning up the bathroom and the kitchen.

Q   Do you know what time he went to bed that night?

A   He came in—it was 11:30. He came in, and he kissed me on the head. He goes, "Are you still feeling bad?" 'Cause he roused me up. It scared me.

Q   This was probably 15 minutes after he tucked you in?

A   Yeah.

Q   When is the next time you saw Wayne?

A   It was about, what, almost 12 o'clock.

Q   That night?

A   Yes.

Q   So you did see him again that night?

A   Yes.

Q It had been about a half hour after he kissed you on top of the head. So you saw him at 12 o'clock. Where was he?

A I started to get up, and I walked into the sitting room 'cause the steers were screaming?

Q The steers were screaming?

A Yeah. And he goes, "You go on back to bed. You're sick. I'll go check on them. I don't want you out in the cold wind." So I turned around and went to bed, and that was the last time I ever seen him.

Q Alive?

A Yes.

Then Janis Bynum told me about the discovery, at about 8:00 the next morning, of her husband lying on his back at the bottom of the stairs, barely conscious, and about she and her daughters carrying him upstairs, about her trying to revive him with wet cloths, about Melvin and Barbara's arrival at about 8:30 in the morning for a barbecue that had been planned for 1 o'clock that afternoon. She also said that when Barbara told her that her husband was hurt real bad, she went to the Dickeys to call for help.

Q How long had the aunt and uncle been there, Barbara and Melvin?

A About five, ten minutes.

Q So if they got there at 8:30 and had been there five or ten minutes when you went to call for help, would that make it maybe quarter of 9:00 or thereabouts?

A Something like that.

Although her time line did not agree with that shown by the 911 records, or those of the squad, the medi-copter crew, the Miami Valley Hospital intake sheet—or for that matter, the statements and/or the testimony of anyone else, I chose not to make an issue of it. It had already become obvious to me that the truth was not in her.

After a short reprise concerning her activities during her husband's final hours, the funeral arrangements, the funeral itself, and her conversations with her children, we moved on:

Q Did you continue to reside in the Dickeys' building?

A No.

Q When did you leave the Dickeys?

A It was three days after he was buried.

Q What happened then?

A My little girl, Erica, she got to where she couldn't sleep in her room no more. I told her, "Okay, baby, you can come sleep with Mommy." And she says, "Mom, Dad's outside." I was like, "No, Dad's not outside." Well, the next day she tried to kill herself.

Q What method did you use to try to kill herself?

A She took a pair of scissors and stabbed herself in the stomach.

Q Did you have to take her to the hospital?

A Yeah, we took her to the hospital in Urbana. The doctor, he put the "butterfly"—it's like tape.

Q Butterfly stitches?

A He goes, well, you know, Dr. Peters, "You don't be doing that. It's going to be okay. You've got to call me. Mommy's got the phone number. Call me." So we decided we're going to get counseling. We're going to get through this.

Q So did you get counseling for her?

A Yeah.

Q And who was the counselor?

A What is his name? John, in Urbana.

Q His name is John?

A Yes. I don't remember his last name right offhand.

Q He's in Urbana?

A Yes, he's in Urbana.

Q How did you come by his name?

A My children was removed from me after their father had died.

Q When was that?

A At the end of July. At the end of July they were removed.

Q Who removed them?

A The State of Ohio.

Q And why did they do that?

A For dependency. I was unstable at the time.

Q What brought it to the attention of the State of Ohio?

A I didn't have a job. I didn't have a place for my children—a permanent place for them to live.

Q Weren't you still living at the Dickeys'?

A No. We moved because my little girl tried to kill herself. We left. She couldn't handle it, and I couldn't handle it.

Q Did I correctly understand you to say you left the Dickeys property three days after the funeral?

A Yes.

Q   Never went back?

A   No.

Q   Did you move all your things?

A   No.

Q   Did you just leave them?

A   Packed a suitcase, and I put it in the vehicle and I left.

Q   Where did you go?

A   At the time I was staying with a friend, what I thought was a friend.

Q   Who was your friend?

A   Mike Nitchman.

Q   And where does he live?

A   In Thackery, Ohio.

Q   How long were you at Mike Nitchman's place?

A   Two to three days.

Q   Then where did you go?

A   Kiser Lake.

Q   What's at Kiser Lake?

A   Nothing. Nothing. That's where I lost my children.

Q   Where did you live at Kiser Lake?

A   In a tent.

Q   One tent?

A   Yes.

Q   This would have been maybe three days after you went to Mike Nitchman's? I'm just trying to get a handle. If you buried Wayne on the 16th of July and three days later you went to Mike Nitchman's, and you stay at Mike's maybe three days?

A   Yes.

Q   And so that would be maybe the 22nd of July you went to
    Kiser Lake?

A   Yes.

Q   You didn't live anyplace else?

A   No.

Q   And who all went?

A   My children.

Q   First to Mike Nitchman's?

A   Me and my children.

Q   What about your mother?

A   She was in an elderly home.

Q   At that time?

A   Yes.

Q   Who placed her there?

A   My brother did. He had come down for a visit
    before Wayne—

Q   Come down?

A   From Georgia. He's like, "Janis, I don't see how you're going to
    take care of her. You know she's not there." And he had filed a
    motion or some kind of motion paperwork thing to place her in an
    elderly home.

Q   So your mother didn't go to Mike Nitchman's?

A   No.

Q   She didn't go to Kiser Lake?

A   No.

Q   It was just you and the three girls—

A   Yes.

Q   —that went to Kiser Lake along about the 22nd day of July?

A   Yes.

Q   And how long did you live in a tent at Kiser Lake?

A   About three weeks to a month.

Q   And then what happened?

A   My children was removed from me.

We then spent perhaps another hour while she claimed to have gotten a job at a Japanese car parts factory located in St. Paris, Ohio. The company was doing business as KTH, and she said she had worked there for ten or eleven months, all the while living with Timothy Stapleton. Then she said she quit that job in order to move to Texas, to retrieve her two oldest children who had, in the interim, been taken to Texas by her husband's parents. Then, when she was refused entry by her erstwhile father-in-law, she was arrested, she said for trespass, but failed to mention the fact that there was already an outstanding warrant for her arrest for violation of her prior order of probation. She told us that she spent nineteen days in jail and somehow came up with $1,090, to finally pay her overdue fine, and was released. She said that while in jail—probably in September of 2000—the State of Texas intervened and assumed custody of the children and she had not seen them since.

She next told us that after she was released from jail, she moved to Lampasas, Texas, and became a nurse's aide. That pretty well brought us up to where we had begun her questioning nearly five hours earlier. Nonetheless, there remained a couple of other items, I wanted to nail down on the record:

Q Have we covered all of the grounds and the various places that you've lived—both before and after your husband died?

A Yes.

Q We haven't missed anything?

A No.

Q You have not remarried?

A No.

Q Do you have a significant other at this point?

A No.

Q Have you had a significant other since your husband died?

A No.

Q So you have not been in residence with a man?

A No.

Q Okay. Who is Mike Warner?

A He was a guy that offered me employment.

Q Was there a time when Mike Warner moved into your house?

A No.

Q Was there a time when you and Mike Warner became intimate?

A No.

Q There was no time when you and Mike Warner and the three children and your mother all lived together in the Dickey House?

A No.

Q Was there a time when you and Mike Warner and your three children and your mother all went to Florida together?

A No.

Q Was there a time when you and Mike Warner and the three children and your mother went to Florida to leave your mother with a relative?

A No.

Q And did a relative come back with you?

A No.

Q And did you have a car break down between Kentucky and Tennessee?

A No.

Q And was it necessary to rent another car to come back?

A No.

Q You indicated that there was a time when you lived in Kiser Lake State Park?

A Yes.

Q Could that possibly have been for a couple of months in November and December of 1999?

A I don't remember. All I know is that we stayed out there, and my children was removed from me.

Q And your mother wasn't with you?

A No.

Q If Mike Warner were to have testified that he lived with you and enjoyed a sexual relationship with you from August of 1999 through January of 2000 and that during that period of time the two of you went to Florida and back and that during that same period of time you lived at Kiser Lake State Park, would that be untrue?

A Yes, it would. Very untrue.

Q If Mike Warner were to have testified on deposition that you told him that your mother pushed your husband down the stairs, would that be true?

A It would not be true. It would be a lie. I love my mother very much.

Q Who is Brian Lansing?

A He's a little teenager boy that was on drugs that lived across from Mike Warner's used furniture store. I thought I could get him off drugs. His dad was abusing him, didn't care.

Q Did you ever tell Brian Lansing that your mother tripped Wayne and pushed him down the stairs?

A No.

Q Do you know who Deb Lansing is?

A Brian's mother.

Q Did you ever tell Deb Lansing in Brian's presence that your mother had pushed Wayne down the stairs?

A No.

Q Did you ever talk with any of the nurses at the care center where your mother ultimately came to live?

A I would talk to them when I couldn't come in, and I would ask them how she's doing, how her state of mind is.

Q Do you remember talking to a Linda Jenkins over there shortly after your husband had died and Linda came up to you and said that she was sorry that you had lost your husband?

A Yes.

Q Did you tell Linda Jenkins that your husband had had a stroke and fallen down the steps and died?

A No, no.

Q I'm looking at a sheriff's call for Service Record, and this is dated November 6 of 1999. It appears to be a call to Kiser Lake camping area for child neglect involving Janis Bynum and refers to a vehicle number with an Ohio license—a 1986 Ford automobile. Does that sound like your vehicle?

A   Yes.

Q   And this would have been in November. And I'm trying to reconcile that with your being there only three weeks beginning in July.

A   It may have been longer that I was out there. I don't know.

Q   The report also refers to a dispatch to Mercy Hospital. Who was at Mercy Hospital?

A   My brother was at the time was out there, and he had my mother.

Q   Didn't they take your mother from that campground to the hospital?

A   I have no idea 'cause I was not speaking to my brother at the time.

Q   Wasn't your mother there in the campground with you?

A   Not at our camp site, no.

Q   Where was she at the park?

A   She was with my brother at another campsite.

And, at that point in her deposition, we revisited some of her earlier testimony:

Q   Do you recall a Leah Conrad of the EMS, emergency medical service, that came out to pick up your husband…

A   There was a woman there, yes.

Q   Do you recall telling her that your husband would occasionally get up and drink alcoholic beverages and then would pass out somewhere on the farm?

A No.

Q Do you recall telling that same person that you had previously found him passed out outside and in the barn or on the porch?

A No.

Q Do you recall telling her that you couldn't find him outside so you went back inside and found him lying on the basement floor at the foot of the steps?

A No. My little girl found her daddy, and started screaming.

Q Do you recall telling this person from Christiansburg EMS that you went downstairs and found him bleeding from the head…

A No.

Q …and so you got a washcloth and cleaned up the injury?

A No.

Q Do you recall telling her or anybody that you were unable to wake him so you left him there to sleep it off?

A No.

Q If you found your husband at 8:00 in the morning, how does it happen that you didn't call 911 until 10:58? That's almost three hours.

A I was trying to see what was wrong with him, and I didn't want to leave him alone.

Q You found Wayne at 8 o'clock?

A Yes.

Q Brought him upstairs?

A It took us awhile to get him upstairs.

Q Then Barbara and Melvin arrived at 8:30?

A Yes.

Q And then it was not until 10:58 that you called 911. Is that correct so far?

A I guess so. I have no idea.

Q Can you give me a better explanation as to what happened between 8:30 when Barbara and Melvin arrived and 10:58 when you finally called 911?

A They kept telling me that he was asleep, you know, that he was drunk.

Q Do you recall telling anybody, after the care flight people had gotten there that you had last seen your husband at 12 o'clock going to the basement to check on a noise?

A No. 'Cause the care flight people came to the room and, you know, asked what was going on. I was like, "I don't know." All I remember is seeing him almost at 12:00 and he was going to check the steers.

Q Do you recall telling them that he had been drinking?

A No. I did not tell them that he was drinking.

Q Do you recall telling one of the nurses that your husband had heard a noise about midnight, thought a neighbor's wolfhound was attacking one of your heifers, so he took a baseball bat and went downstairs to check?

A No. We never had kept baseball bats, guns or anything in the house.

Q You didn't have a baseball bat in the house?

A No.

Q Did you two have any arguments that day before this happened...

A No.

Q   …that Saturday afternoon?

A   No.

Q   Was there an occasion when you were outside and you actually got physical, you had a physical fight?

A   No.

Q   And at some time he actually fell down and you jumped on him?

A   No.

Q   And he got frustrated and struck the window of his car?

A   He kicked his car 'cause I told him that I didn't want a bunch of company over late at night. He kicked the side of his black car, yes.

Q   Okay. So you did at least have an argument?

A   No. It was not an argument. It was my opinion.

Q   If I have testimony from witnesses who say they saw you strike him and actually get on top of him when he was on the ground, you would disagree with that?

A   Yes, I would.

Q   Are you aware that there are people in your husband's family who believe that you killed your husband?

A   Yes.

Q   Who are those people?

A   His brother, his mother, his father. You know, the whole family. His aunts, his uncles.

Q   Do you know why they've reached that conclusion?

A   'Cause they hate my guts.

Q   Are you aware that your mother has said that the two of you had gotten into an argument—a rather loud argument and that you pushed him down the stairs?

A No.

Q Are you aware that Mike Warner has testified that you told him that your mother did it?

A No. That's not true because...

Q Did you ever introduce Mike Warner as your fiancé?

A No.

Q Have you been pregnant at any time since your husband's death?

A No.

Q So you wouldn't have told one of the nurses that you were pregnant?

A I can't have children.

And then, finally, just before we terminated her deposition, I wanted to clear up a couple more matters—more as a matter of curiosity than anything else. The first such matter confirmed a suspicion that both Dick Rice and I had discussed during a short break in the proceedings:

Q Have you had sexual relations with any man since your husband died?

A I've had one boyfriend, yes.

Q And who is that?

A Dewayne Bullard.

Q And who is he?

A Miss Estep's grandson.

Q Is he the gentleman who is waiting in the reception room?

A Yes.

Q   And in point of fact, you brought Miss Estep and Dewayne...?

A   Yes, Bullard.

Q   Are you engaged to him?

A   Yes.

The second matter I wanted her to clarify concerned her decision to sue the Dickeys:

Q   You don't really know how your husband died, do you?

A   No, I don't. And I fight with this nightmare after nightmare after nightmare. I wake up screaming, you know why?

Q   Okay. Why? And I'm not sure you've answered my question, which is how did you come to the decision to sue Mr. and Mrs. Dickey?

A   Because I lost my soul-mate, my husband. She has her husband. She has her father to her children. My children has no father.

Q   Tie that up for me.

A   If she would have put the handrail down there like she had promised to do, my husband might have been alive.

Q   But we don't know that, do we?

A   No. And my...

Q   So why have you decided to sue her?

A   In my heart I believe that if that handrail was there he might have been a vegetable, but he would have still been alive and I would still be here taking care of him.

Janis Bynum's deposition had lasted more than five hours and had been extraordinarily tedious; it was adjourned at 3:40 that afternoon and she and Mr. Daly left the conference chamber immediately. Dick Rice and I remained to critique her testimony—

and to await news of Janis' arrest by the sheriff's deputies who had patiently awaited her release from the deposition.

"Well, John," Dick couldn't resist a wry grin. "I guess that blows your 'ball bat' theory; I distinctly heard her say they'd never had one in the house."

"You'll pardon me, I hope, if I don't accept anything she told us as truthful. In fact, based on the over-all veracity of her testimony, I'd be willing to bet

Janis Bynum's mugshot

that there were half a dozen ball-bats in their home. In fact, I think she may well have confirmed the accuracy of my 'figure of speech' surmise about her having ball-batted or tire-ironed him."

He affected a look of mock disbelief, and asked, "You don't think her testimony was entirely truthful?"

"Do I really have to answer that?" I replied sardonically.

"No," he said. "I think I can work that one out by myself."

"Alright then," I remarked. "Now, in a more serious vein, what did you make of all her testimony?"

He just shook his head. "Seems like everybody we talk to has a different version, both as to what happened that night and the following morning, and as to Janis' activities after her husband's funeral. I get the feeling that we've heard an entire panoply of vast discrepancies in the testimony of virtually everyone we've talked with—as well as with the written records we've seen from the squad, the care-flight personnel and the hospital charts. Whose story are we to believe?"

"I'm not sure it really matters," I answered. "I'm inclined to credit all of the written records; they were all created by disinterested persons in the ordinary course of performing their respective duties. There would have been no motivation on their part to falsify, or to invent, or even to moderate what they recorded.

"I'm also inclined to believe what we've heard from those other witnesses who really have no obvious motive to deliberately misstate or misrepresent anything to which they have attested. That, of course would include Linda Jenkins, the nurse at the Urbana Care Center, and Debbie Lansing, Brian's mother."

Dick nodded, "I agree with that assessment," he said. "What do you think about the three kids?"

"Actually," I said. "I thought they were both candid and truthful to the best of their recollections; I recognize that there were minor differences in their stories, but not in any particular that I considered to be significant—which is what I would expect. After all, they're young kids, and I wouldn't have expected their separately-taken depositions to be entirely consistent in every respect."

"And Mike Warner?" Dick asked pointedly.

"Frankly, I'm inclined to believe his testimony also." I added. "Clearly, there is a vast difference between what he told us last October and that which we just heard from Janis, but I find his testimony to be far more credible than the demonstratively obvious lies which she told us today."

At about that point in our discussion, I heard and responded to a squawk on the intercom in the corner of our conference room. It was Cindy Nash, our receptionist, who told me that Mr. Daly was still in our reception room and had insisted that she tell me that he wanted me to come out and speak with him. That event, I confess, was not wholly unanticipated. Both Dick and I had been speculating about Mr. Daly's anticipated reaction when he—and his client—would discover that they had been waylaid by two Miami County Sheriff's deputies, and his client escorted to the county jail for detention and interrogation. And, of course, I told her I'd be right up.

I appeared within less than a minute and was greeted by a very exercised Mr. Daly, who met me with an angry visage and an equally angry, "Goddamit, John, you sandbagged me! That was a rotten stunt, and I consider it to be wholly unprofessional on your part."

"Hold on a minute, Bill," I responded. "What is it you think I've done that you believe to be unprofessional?"

"You know damn well what I'm talking about," he raved. "You had two deputies sitting here for the express purpose of arresting my client as soon as you'd finished her deposition. You might have warned me about it, and you didn't. You let me—and my client—walk right into a trap. That's what I call a sandbag operation!"

"Alright," I said. "Lets talk about that a minute, okay? The sheriff's office has wanted to talk with your client about her husband's death—and they had an outstanding warrant out of Champaign County for her arrest on a bad check charge. They didn't know where she could be located and asked me if I had any knowledge concerning her whereabouts. Had I not told them that I expected her to be here today for her deposition, I would have been guilty of obstruction of justice."

"Mmhuh," he responded dubiously.

"You're not suggesting that I somehow owed you and/or your client an obligation to place myself in that position, are you?" I asked.

"Well, no," he conceded. "But you made her come here for deposition, knowing that she would be arrested."

"So?" I countered. "I'm entitled to take her deposition. In fact, it's my duty to my client to take her deposition. She caused this action to be filed against my clients, and having done so, she has an affirmative duty under the Rules to appear and answer concerning the allegations of her Complaint. You know that as well as I do. The Court would never force me to trial without first affording me the opportunity to depose her. That's pretty elementary."

He shifted his weight from foot to foot, presumably trying to decide what more to say by way of further argument.

"So what do you think I've done that was 'unprofessional?'" I asked.

"Okay," he finally conceded. "But I still don't like it."

"You don't have to like it, Bill," I offered. "She put herself in that situation, you didn't."

After Mr. Daly left the office, I was surprised to note that he turned to walk south from my office, rather than north towards the sheriff's office and the county jail. I had expected him to rejoin his client in order to be present for her interview with the deputies and to arrange for her release on bail on the bad check charge. (I later came to understand that he did return later that evening—after Janis had been booked on the bad check warrant—and posted bond for her release so that she, Dewayne Bullard and Miss Estep could make good their return to Texas.)

Upon my return to the conference room, I reported my conversation with Mr. Daly to Dick Rice, much to his amusement. "Well," he said drolly, "you did kinda mouse-trap him."

"Yeah, I guess maybe I did," I conceded. "But let's agree that he and his client made it necessary to depose her, and that I had an affirmative duty to notify the sheriff's office where they might find her. I certainly did nothing unprofessional."

"Oh, I couldn't agree more. We had to depose her—and since you knew of her whereabouts, I think you had a duty to advise the deputies," he chortled. "But I do think it's kinda funny—and she certainly did put her own head in there."

Then we reverted to our earlier reprise of Janis' testimony. "A little while ago, when we were talking about all the lies we heard from Janis today and the various discrepancies in the testimony of some of the other witnesses, you said you didn't think it really matters who's lying and who's telling the truth. Educate me on that score, would you?"

"That one's easy," I said. "The Complaint filed in this action contains an entire plethora of pure bullshit, as we've previously recognized. But the whole case stands or falls on her ability to prove by a preponderance of the evidence that her husband fell down the cellar steps because they were defective. But she has no testimony, from anyone, that he actually fell down the steps; what's more, she herself just confessed, under oath, that we don't really know how he died. She said only that if there had been a handrail in place, he might have been still alive; but when I asked her, 'But we don't really know that, do we?' She answered 'No.'

"She acknowledges that she did not see him fall; and, by the same token there is no one else who has any real knowledge that he actually did fall. No one saw him fall—if, in fact, he fell at all. She can probably convince someone that he was found at the bottom of the steps in a moribund condition and thereby give rise to an inference that he fell, tripped, slipped or was pushed down the steps, but even so, that's a long way from showing, by a preponderance of all the evidence, that his death resulted from some negligence or fault on the part of the Dickeys."

"Gotcha," Dick agreed.

"Add to that—unnecessarily—the fact that she has just demonstrated that she is a pathological liar, probably congenital as well; I can't imagine she could convince a jury that the earth is round."

"Yeah, she does seem to have some difficulty with the truth," Dick agreed. "So what do we do now?"

"Let me call Steve Lord tomorrow, see what developed from their interview, and then let's talk about it again," I answered. "I've got some ideas."

I could scarcely wait to talk with Deputy Steve Lord the following morning. I called him at my first opportunity. He told me that they had spent a long evening with Janis Bynum, during which they took a full statement from her and, with her consent, administered a computerized voice stress analysis. She did admit to having lied to me during her deposition, specifically in her denials that she and Mike Warner had lived together, journeyed to Florida together and stayed at Kiser Lake together. She also admitted that she "strongly suspected" her mother of causing her husband's death. On that subject, she told Sergeant Lord, "I lied because she was my mom." She also told him that she lied to everybody in an attempt to find out what had happened to Doug, and that she didn't think the lawsuit should have been filed. "I don't want the damn settlement," she said. "I did not want to file the lawsuit."

As for the voice stress analysis, Steve said, "she really did pretty well."

"So," I queried. "Where are we now?"

"John," he answered. "I really think she did it, but we don't have the evidence to prove it. We had to let her go. We're not closing the file yet; something might turn up, but we can't charge her on what we have so far. We did hold her on the warrant from Champaign County, but that's about all we can do with what we have now."

All of which, I fully understood and agreed with. I then called Dick Rice to bring him up to speed. Both of us admitted to considerable surprise at her having passed the voice stress analysis, because we believed that despite her admission that she had lied on deposition, there were still a great many untruths in the story she had told to the deputies. However we agreed that the voice stress tests were probably no more reliable than were lie detector exams; neither of the tests were consistently infallible.

"So, where do we go from here?" he asked.

"I've got some ideas on that subject," I answered. "Rather obviously, we can take a couple more depositions, like that of Melvin and Barbara Bynum, some of the Champaign County Deputies, Timothy Stapleton, et cetera, and then, based on what we already have and those additional depositions, we can file a Motion for Summary Judgment. I strongly believe the Court would grant the Motion and dismiss the action against the Dickeys, with prejudice, and it's over. In the unlikely event that the Court should deny the Motion, we'll try the case to a jury in October.

"Or," I continued, "I can call Daly, remind him of the evidence that we have—and the evidence and proofs that he doesn't have—and offer him a sop to pack it in and settle his case for its nuisance value."

"What amount do you have in mind. What's nuisance value in this case?" Dick asked.

"I'd be willing to bet he'd jump at $2,500." I said. "He's got to know there's no way in hell he can prove any of the elements of his case. For him, it's a lead-pipe loser, and I'll be greatly surprised if he hasn't figured that out by now.

"Something else we need to think about is the fact that taking two or three more depositions, then preparing and filing a Motion for Summary Judgment, with attachments and a Brief in Support, is very likely going to add another six to eight thousand dollars to the cost of defense—and, in the unthinkable event that the Court should miss a beat and fail to sustain our Motion, and we actually have to go to trial—you're looking at another eight to ten thousand more."

"Makes sense to me," Dick said. "If you can get it done. Do you really think Daly—and his client—would accept that kind of peanuts in full settlement?"

"I'd bet on it," I said. "Want me to give it a shot?"

"If you think it has a chance, I sure do. The Company will be happy to save the money," he answered quickly.

"Let's let him stew awhile, let him evaluate his case on his own—which I'm sure he'll do as we get closer to the trial date. He might even ask us what we'd be willing to settle for—and if he doesn't, I'll initiate a discussion on the subject of settlement. Okay with you?"

"Suits me fine; you're driving," he said.

Some weeks later, Mr. Daly and I had that conversation; I frankly do not remember whether he called me or vice versa, but we mutually acknowledged that the discovery cutoff date, the time for witness and exhibit exchange, the last date for the filing of a Motion for Summary Judgment, and, most importantly, the trial date were fast approaching. There was also an unspoken acknowledgment that, based on his total lack of evidence as to the cause of Doug (or Wayne) Bynum's death, and his client's open admission of that fact—coupled, of course, with his client's total lack of candor, her repeated and demonstrable untruths concerning the event of her husband's death and her own seemingly wanton activities afterward, et cetera, et cetera—he might well have some little difficulty in establishing the Dickeys' liability by a preponderance of all the evidence.

Although we spent considerable telephone time in discussing the pros and cons of the matter, I finally got his agreement to settle the case for the grand sum of $1,200.

"You'll want to discuss that with your client," I suggested.

And he replied, "Not necessary. I already have; she'll take it. And, at least, that will enable me to recover some small part of my costs advanced."

"All right," I agreed. "You'll need to get the approval of the Probate Court to settle on that basis; since you're counsel for the estate, I'll look to you for that. I'll prepare a general release and a dismissal entry, with prejudice to all parties. When we get all that done, I'll have a check ready. Okay?"

"Sounds good to me," he said. "I'll start on my part right away. As you know, it'll take some time for me to garner signatures from Janis and from Jeff Livingston, as well as from the guardians for the two girls."

"And I'll have my documents—and the check ready when you've received your Court approval," I assured him.

"Twelve hundred!" Dick fairly whooped. "How the hell did you get that done?"

"I'd like to be able to tell you it was hard work," I said. "But it was rather easily done. I think that both Mr. Daly and his client could see the handwriting on the wall. They simply had no single shred of evidence with which to sustain the allegations of their Complaint. Add to that basic, immutable truth, the fact that Janis' own testimony would have been a totally humiliating disaster, especially on cross, and you can see why both of them would be eager to have it over and done with—once and for all.

"And, I'd be willing to bet she'll never be seen in Ohio again," I concluded.

It did, indeed, take a bit of time to get the paper work completed, but the matter was finally concluded, with Probate Court approval, and a final judgment entry of dismissal was approved and filed with the Common Pleas Court on August 1, 2001. It was finally over.

Dick Rice and I celebrated the conclusion of the litigation over a cup of his office coffee, which I had previously conceded to be better than we brewed in my office. Our reprise of the case and our celebration ended with his final remark and my own response.

"Well now, John," he said. "You've written a number of books about Miami County murder cases. You've got to write this one."

"Not me, Bud," I answered him. "This case involved a civil claim for damages. It wasn't a murder case."

"The hell it wasn't," he rejoined. "Do you have any doubt she killed him?"

"Not really," I replied. "But she was never charged—or tried—for it. Besides that, I really don't have either the time or the energy to tackle this one. At least, not now."

EPILOGUE

After the case had been settled, and I had been paid my final billing for attorney fees and costs incurred in the defense of Miami Mutual's insureds, Warren and Edra Dickey, I closed my file and moved on to other matters.

It was not until much later that I learned that the Miami County Sheriff's Office had come by further information concerning the death of Douglas Wayne Bynum. It seems that more than a year after our case had been terminated, Sergeant Steve Lord received a telephone call from a Crystal Bynum, Doug Bynum's sister-in-law, and matters progressed from there. Steve Lord was good enough to allow me to copy his investigative log. I have presented the entries which appear in that log, beginning with reference to a telephone call from Crystal Bynum:

On or about August 30, 2002, Crystal Bynum, PO Box 241, Limp Pass, TX, (512) 556-3018, SSN: 465-89-0689, DOB: 05-19-79 who is the deceased's sister-in-law called regarding the investigation. She stated that Janis Bynum does not have her children and that Children Protective Services has them due to her having them living in an unfit environment. Crystal stated that Janis' daughters Erica and Holly have told her (Crystal) that they suspect that their mother killed their father.

On or about November 4, 2002, Crystal Bynum called and told me that Erica Bynum, 13 years of age, had told her foster-mother, Patricia Swift, 4202 Odelia Dr., Killeen, Texas, 76524, (254) 699-6201, that she had observed her mother, Janis Bynum, hit Wayne Bynum with a baseball bat. Crystal Bynum stated that Swift advised that Erica saw Janis Bynum hit Wayne Bynum in the head with a baseball bat. She also advised that Michael Warner was at the house the night Wayne Bynum was injured. Crystal Bynum stated that Warner may have assisted in the assault which led to Wayne Bynum's death. She communicated that the baseball bat used to hit Wayne Bynum had been thrown in a lake. Crystal Bynum stated that Erica Bynum had told Swift that Janis Bynum and Michael Warner put Wayne Bynum at the bottom of the stairs to make it appear that he had fallen. Crystal Bynum explained that she had observed baseball bats in the Bynum residence. Crystal Bynum explained that she had learned that Janis and Wayne Bynum had been arguing earlier in the day about Wayne learning that Michael Warner and Janis Bynum were having an affair. Crystal Bynum communicated that she had been told that Wayne Bynum had confronted Michael Warner at his antique shop about the affair. She stated that Wayne Bynum had threatened Warner. Crystal Bynum advised that this was two days before Wayne Bynum was injured. Crystal Bynum advised that Erica Bynum had lied about the matter because her mother had threatened to kill her if she told anyone.

Tape of phone call

On or about November 5, 2002 Bob Clark of Children's Service of Bernn, Texas, (512) 715-3535, called and told me that Erica Bynum had made a disclosure to her foster mother, Patricia Swift, that she had observed her mother kill her father with a baseball bat. Bob Clark stated that the State of Texas was the official parent of Erica Bynum. Clark stated that Emily Klutts is Erica Bynum's assigned caseworker (512) 715-3533. Clark encouraged contacting the foster mother and having Erica Bynum interviewed.

Tape of phone call

On or about November 6, 2002 Patricia Swift stated the following during a tape-recorded telephone conversation. She learned the following information from Erica Bynum regarding the death of her father. Swift advised that Erica doesn't want to see her mother and wanted no contact with her. She explained that Erica had been emotional about her father's upcoming birthday. Swift stated she had a conversation with Erica told her that she had a secret she couldn't live with any longer. Swift advised that Erica told her that she was afraid to talk about it because she had lied to her family, specifically her sister regarding knowing about how her father died. Swift explained that Erica told her that her mother, Janis Bynum, made her go get her a baseball bat. Erica told Swift that Mike Warner was at the house and Janis Bynum had her bring her an aluminum baseball bat. Swift stated that Erica told her that she saw the bat being swung and her father being struck in the upstairs not in the basement. Swift advised that Erica advised that she went to her room crying and found her father the next morning at the foot of the stairs in the basement. Erica told Swift that she lied because her mother threatened to kill her. An interview is being arranged with the Killeen, Texas Police Department with Erica to take an official statement.

Tape of phone call

On or about November 7, 2002, Erica Bynum gave an official statement to Investigator Faes of the Killeen, Texas Police Department regarding her knowledge of the death of her father. She stated that on or about July 10, 1999 her mother had opened a screen door and hit her with it. Erica advised that it was an accident and that she started to cry. She explained that her mother and father began arguing about the matter. Erica communicated that her father punched a car window in frustration during the argument. Erica stated that a fist fight broke out between her mother and father. Erica advised that her mother had to be pulled off of her father. She communicated that later that night her father was drinking beer and taking aspirin., Erica stated that her sisters went to bed at approximately 2300 hours. She advised that approximately fifteen minutes later she went to bed in her mother's room. Erica advised that she routinely slept with her mother and that her father slept on the couch. She stated that she heard her grandmother go to bed and that her mom came into the bedroom. Erica advised that her mother laid down, but kept her clothes on. She explained that her mother got up approximately twenty minutes later. Erica stated that she heard a car door close and had heard her mother get out of bed. Erica articulated that she went into the livingroom where her dad was sleeping on the couch. She stated that she saw her mother and Michael Warner standing in front of the couch. Erica explained that she knew Warner from being at his shop with his mother and his having delivered a washer to the house. Erica explained that her mother and Warner were arguing and were talking about hitting him (her father). Erica stated that she asked her mother what they were arguing about. She advised that her mother told her to go away. Erica stated that she asked her mother what they were doing. She communicated that her mother told her to go get her a softball bat. Erica stated that she was afraid of her mother hitting her so she went and got the bat. She advised that the bat was metal and was blue in color. **Erica** explained that her mother took the bat. She articulated that her father was asleep on the couch lying on his stomach. **Erica** stated that from a distance of about five feet she could see someone swinging the bat and striking her father. She advised that her father was struck on the head with the bat. **Erica** communicated that she saw at least three swings of the bat. She stated that the only people in the room were her father, **Warner** and her mother. **Erica** explained that she saw her mother and **Warner** carry her dad from the couch. She advised that **Warner** had him by his shoulders and her mother had a hold of her father's feet. **Erica** communicated that they were carrying him towards the basement. **Erica** stated that she ran to her room and got into bed. She explained that she did not hear anything else that night. **Erica** stated that the next morning around 0800 hours that she heard her mother calling her father's name. She said that she went downstairs and found her mother on the steps outside. **Erica** advised that she asked her mother what she was doing and was told that she was looking for her father. **Erica** stated that she could see her father lying at the foot of the basement floor. She stated that her mother told her to wake her sisters so as they could help carry their father up the stairs. **Erica** advised that they all went into the basement. She explained that her father was lying on his back with his arms crossed on his chest. **Erica** stated that she saw dried blood on the right side of her father's face. She stated that her father vomited when they tried to move him upstairs. **Erica** advised that once they got him upstairs that her mother splashed ice water on his face attempting to keep him awake. **Erica** stated that her mother was trying to feed her father. She stated that her Uncle Melvin arrived and an ambulance was called for her father. **Erica** advised that her father was taken to the hospital by a helicopter. She stated that she stayed home with her grandmother and didn't go to the hospital. **Erica** communicated that her mother came home from the hospital that night and asked her if she saw what happened to her father. She stated that she told her mother yes, I remember. **Erica** stated that her mother told her if she ever told anyone what she saw that she would kill her. She advised that her mother threatened her in a mean tone and she told her she would say nothing. **Erica** stated that **Warner** began coming to the house while her father was in the hospital. She articulated that **Warner** began staying at the house a few days after her father's funeral. She stated that he would stay in her parent's room with her mother. **Erica** stated that it was approximately one week after the funeral when her mother showed her an engagement ring from **Warner**. **Erica** stated that they went to Florida with **Warner** when they could no longer pay the rent. She stated that they came back to Ohio and stayed at Kiser Lake in tents. **Erica** advised that her mother was with **Warner** and would stop in periodically to check on them. She stated that Children's Services put them in foster-care once the police found out they were living in tents. **Erica** admitted not telling the truth during her deposition. **Erica** concluded her statement by advising that her mother was closest to her father with the bat and that she was probably the person delivering the blows. She stated that she didn't see her father fall down the stairs.

Statement of Erica Bynum

On or about November 21, 2002, Dr. Lehman a Forensic Pathologist at the Montgomery County Coroner's Office stated the following after reviewing his findings of the autopsy he performed on **Wayne Bynum**. Dr. Lehman was given the background on the case to include the recent statement given by **Erica Bynum** that she saw her father hit with a bat by her mother. Dr. Lehman stated that if an individual strikes their head on a flat surface they are less likely to split their scalp or cause a blunt force laceration. He **stated** that it is very likely if a person was hit with a bat or an object that was round and hard like a bat that a blunt force scalp laceration would be present. He noted that **Wayne Bynum** didn't have a scalp laceration. Dr. Lehman stated that **Wayne Bynum** received a very good blow because he had a very large skull fracture. He explained that a bat would tend to give a person a depressed skull fracture which was absent with **Wayne Bynum**. Dr. Lehman articulated that a large flat surface tends to be responsible for a linear skull fracture which **Wayne Bynum** experienced. Dr. Lehman stated that he couldn't exclude that **Wayne Bynum** was hit with a bat, but he indicated that the story of the fall down the stairs was more consistent with the injury. Dr. Lehman stated that a metal baseball bat should have split the scalp open especially if someone was hit hard enough to cause a skull fracture. Dr. Lehman stated that it was more likely that the injury was caused by a fall, but he couldn't eliminate that a bat may have been used to cause the injury. He indicated that he found it odd that **Janis Bynum** had indicated that her husband had been drinking all day, but no alcohol was detected during the toxicology. Dr. Lehman said that he found this suspicious. He advised that the injuries were consistent with a fall. He noted the skull fracture on the left side and the brain contusion and bleeding on the right. Dr. Lehman stated that this was typical of a fall where you have an impact injury on one side and internal injuries on the opposite side of the head. He stated that a typical blow with a bat usually all the injuries are under the blow. Dr. Lehman advised that all the injuries are under the blow such as the skull fracture and the brain contusion. Dr. Lehman indicated that he may have been initially hit with a bat and then tumbled down the stairs. He stated that if the bat injury wasn't serious and he was thrown down the stairs the injuries may have been sustained in that manner.

On or about January 4, 2003 Crystal Bynum relayed information that **Warren Dickey** had a blue metal baseball bat which had been found in the **Bynum** home after **Janice Bynum** had moved out. Sgt. Emrick responded to 7456 East State Route 55, Casstown and picked up the bat from **Warren Dickey**. The bat was placed into evidence.

On or about January 6, 2003 **Warren Dickey** communicated that he had previously spoken to the Bynum family in Texas and they had inquired if he had found a bat in the house Wayne and his family had been living. **Dickey** explained that he had discovered that **Janice Bynum** had abandoned the house and all of their property was left behind. He stated that he gave the new tenant, **Ken McAlister**, a few months of free rent to clean up the mess. **Dickey** advised that he asked **McAlister** if he had found a bat. **Dickey** stated that **McAlister** told him that he had found a bat and that his son was using it to play baseball. **Dickey** indicated that he has had the bat for approximately four months. He stated that he has been calling the Bynum family to tell them about the bat, but was unable to reach them until January 4, 2003. **Ken McAlister** was spoken to on his cellular phone, (937) 238-5371 and he advised that he found the bat in the house. He indicated that he recalled that baseball equipment was kept on a shelf at a top of the basement stairs. **McAlister** advised he couldn't recall where he had found the bat, but he had given it to his son to play baseball. He stated that he had retrieved the bat from his son and turned it over to **Warren Dickey**. **McAlister** stated that he repainted and carpeted the living room. He advised that he would permit lab technicians into the home to examine it for forensic evidence. The bat was taken to the lab for analysis.

Although not mentioned in the log itself, the department files also contained an affidavit given by Holly Bynum at the end of December, 2002 which reads as follows:

KILLEEN POLICE DEPARTMENT

STATE OF TEXAS

VOLUNTARY STATEMENT - (NOT UNDER ARREST)

THE STATE OF TEXAS   CASE: 02-014138   TIME 10:30AM

COUNTY OF BELL   OFFICER: FAES

Before me, the undersigned authority in and for the said County and State, on this December 30, 2002, personally appeared:

NAME: Holly A. Bynum
D.O.B.: 08-05-87
SSN: 463-87-3141
HOME ADDRESS: Rt. 1 Box 65, Mullin, TX 76864
HOME PHONE: 915-985-3521
SCHOOL: Mullen High School
GUARDIAN: Pamela Greer

Who voluntarily makes the following statement: Back in 1999, I was living in Troy, Ohio with my mom, Janis, my dad, Douglas Wayne, my grandma, Dorothy Price, and my two sisters, Amanda and Erica. We lived in a two story house with a basement. In July, sometime in the beginning of the week, we were outside. Amanda and I were mowing the lawn. We started to argue. Mom came outside. She opened the door really wide. She hit Erica in the back with the door. Erica was crying. That is when dad came outside and started to argue with my mom. They got into a fist fight. My mom kept hitting my dad. My mom threatened to bust out his car windows. My dad tried to bust out his windows with his fist. My dad hurt his hand. Me and Amanda thought that he broke his hand. My mom and dad finally stopped arguing. Everyone went inside. Me, Amanda and my dad stayed in the dining room listening to music. We stayed in there for hours until night came around. I went into my mom's room. It was dark outside. I was talking to my mom. My dad came in there and told me to get out, so he could go to sleep. I went into Erica's room. Erica was already in the room. She was not sleeping. She was just laying there. I slept on the floor. I fell asleep. The next morning, she woke me up. I did not get up during the night. She wanted me to help carry our dad up from the basement. She said that he had fallen down the stairs. Me and Amanda went to the stairs. He was laying on the floor. He was unconscious. Amanda told us not to move him because he might be hurt real bad. My mom told us to pick him up and move him anyway. My dad's head was laying by the stairs. His arms were by his side. To me, it did not look like he had fallen down the stairs. His position did not look right. If someone had fallen down the stairs, he would not have landed like that. I don't remember seeing any bruises. I remember seeing a gash in the back of his head. We carried him up the stairs. He started to wake up. We layed him down on the floor in the dining room. We tried to talk to him. He would not wake up. Something was wrong that day. Our mom had already cooked breakfast for us. She told us that he had fallen during the night after drinking a lot. She said that he mistook the basement door for the outside door. It did not seem right that my mom would be cooking breakfast while our dad was laying on the basement floor. She did not call an ambulance. She did not call the ambulance until my dad's uncle arrived that day. That was about an hour and a half later. My dad just layed on the dining room floor. I splashed water on his face. My mom was telling him to get up. Melvin Bynum and his wife showed up. They said that my mom needed to go call the ambulance. She was telling them that my dad would wake up. They had to tell her two or three times to get an ambulance. We did not have a phone. My mom drove to the landlord's house. I was with her. We called for an ambulance from their house. My mom was not really upset that morning. The ambulance came. They brought a helicopter. They life-flighted my dad to the hospital. My dad stayed in the hospital for about two days. My dad died in the hospital. He never woke up. My dad was not able to tell us what happened. I don't know what happened. My mom had a boyfriend, Mike Warner, not even two weeks after my dad died. My mom and dad bought a washer and dryer from him before my dad died. It was about a week before my dad died. Mike did not deliver the washer and dryer like he was suppose to. My dad had gone up to his shop with a baseball bat. I think that my dad threatened Mike that day. My dad came home. I think that it was the next day that the washer and dryer got delivered to the house. Mike brought them to our house. My dad was home. Mike dropped them off then left. My mom was home that day. She did not say anything. I never saw Mike again until after my dad died. Mike moved into our house about a couple of weeks after my dad died. The night that my dad got hurt, I was in my sister's bedroom. I went to sleep first. I did not wake up during the night. In the morning, she got up first. I don't know what happened that night. I have heard what my sister is saying. I believe that she saw something that night, but I don't know if it happened exactly like she is saying. I think that my mom is capable of hurting my dad. When we were growing up, they had fist fights all of the time. My dad would not hit my mom back. We would call our grandmother and grandfather to come help. They would pull my mom off of our dad. My mom has bragged that she pulled a knife on our dad and stabbed him. This was before I was born, so I don't know if it really happened. I had never seen her use any weapons when she had been fighting with my dad. I don't think that Erica is making this up. Erica was mom's baby. Even after dad died, they were still close. Erica and I had the same father. Amanda is my half-sister. She has a different dad. Amanda has never said anything about our dad dying. My grandmother, Dorothy Price, was in the house the night that my dad died. She had said that she was up dancing with my dad until 1:00am. That was not truth unless he woke up. He went to bed before that. Grandma Price would not say anything if she saw mom hurt dad. I don't even remember seeing her the next day when dad was hurt. I think that she was in her room. She was in a wheel chair. She told people that she could not walk, but she really could. I had seen her walk without the wheel chair. My mom made us move after our dad died. She said that it was a vacation, but it wasn't. We had to live in a tent. C.P.S. picked us up. They let us go back home after my mom got a house and a job. I have never been back to that house. There were baseball bats in our house

Holly Bynum

when my dad died. Us girls all played softball. I did not see the baseball bats after my dad died. The reason why I am making this statement today is because I did not tell everything I knew when I made the first statement to the man in the courthouse. I still wanted to stay with my mother back then and did not say anything that would stop us from going back to live with her. Everything that I have said today is the truth. This happened right before my 12th birthday. I am fifteen years old at the time of my statement.

THE ABOVE STATEMENT IS TRUE AND CORRECT TO THE BEST OF MY KNOWLEDGE. I AM 15 YEARS OLD AND I DO READ AND WRITE THE ENGLISH LANGUAGE. I COMPLETED THE 8th GRADE IN PUBLIC SCHOOLS. I HAVE NOT BEEN PROMISED ANYTHING OR THREATENED IN ANY MANNER TO CAUSE ME TO GIVE THIS STATEMENT. THIS OFFENSE DID OCCUR IN THE CITY OF KILLEEN, BELL COUNTY, TEXAS.

signature

SWORN TO AND SUBSCRIBED TO BEFORE ME ON THIS THE 26 DAY OF DECEMBER, 2002 A.D.

Notary Public in and
for the State of Texas

The baseball bat turned in by Mr. McAlister was sent by Sergeant Lord to the Miami Valley Regional Crime Laboratory for analysis, but the results were inconclusive. The correspondence concerning the aluminum bat are shown here:

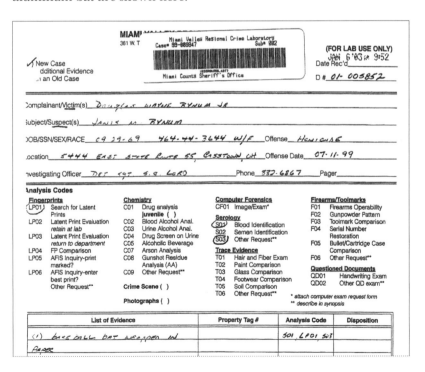

ynopsis of Case: _BASEBALL BAT MAY HAVE BEEN UTILIZED AS WEAPON CAUSING_
BLUNT FORCE TRAUMA TO VICTIM. ANALYZE FOR BLOOD AND HAIR EVIDENCE
LATENT PRINT EXAMINATION IF POSSIBLE AFTER CHECKING FOR blood + hair.

ubmitting Officer _SGT. S. C. LORD_ _____ Department _MICSO_ _____ Phone (937) 332-4867
ddress _201 W. MAIN_ _____ City _TROY_ _____ Zip _45377_ FAX _335-5808_

NATIONALLY ACCREDITED BY THE AMERICAN SOCIETY OF CRIME LABORATORY DIRECTORS/LABORATORY ACCREDITATION BOARD

_____Admin Review

Miami Valley Regional Crime Laboratory

361 West Third Street, Dayton, Ohio 45402
Phone (937) 225-4990   FAX (937) 496-7916
Kenneth M. Betz, Director

TO: Sergeant Steve Lord   January 23, 2003
        Miami County Sheriff's Office

SUBJECT: Laboratory Case 99-009847 - Death occurring at 5444 SR55 on July 11, 1999 (Agency Case #
          01-5852)

          Complainant: BYNUM, JR., DOUGLAS WAYNE
          Subject: BYNUM, JANIS M.

The following evidence was received by the Laboratory for analysis:

Submission 002:   One brown paper package containing one aluminum baseball bat

RESULTS AND CONCLUSIONS

Serological analysis of the bat failed to indicate the presence of blood. No apparent hairs were noted.

The evidence has been forwarded to the Latent Print Section.

Respectfully,

Annette E. Davis
Forensic Scientist

Miami Valley Regional Crime Laboratory

361 West Third Street, Dayton, Ohio 45402
Phone (937) 225-4990   FAX (937) 496-7916
Kenneth M. Betz, Director

TO: Sergeant Steve Lord   April 24, 2003
      Miami County Sheriff's Office

SUBJECT: Laboratory Case 99-009847 - Death occurring at 5444 SR55 on July 11, 1999 (Agency Case # 01-5852)

          Complainant: BYNUM, JR., DOUGLAS WAYNE
          Subject: BYNUM, JANIS M.

The following evidence was received by the Laboratory for analysis:

Submission 002: One brown paper package containing one aluminum baseball bat

RESULTS AND CONCLUSIONS

The evidence in Submission #2 was processed for latent prints and latent prints of value were developed for comparison purposes and for AFIS entry.

One latent print of value was entered into the Automated Fingerprint Identification System with negative results.

There are no prints on file at the lab for the suspect, Janis Bynum, SSN: 464-44-3644. Please obtain a set of case prints (which includes fingerprints and palmprints) and resubmit this case for comparison.

The latent prints developed in this case will be retained on file at the lab under Submission #3.

Submission #2 is available for pickup.

Respectfully,

Aaron A. Davies
Latent Print Technician

Ronald L. Huston
Latent Fingerprint Examiner

AUTHOR'S NOTE

I found this case to be somewhat unique, in that an investigation which had been instigated by an insurance company to determine the merits of Janis Bynum's civil suit for damages sustained by reason of the Dickeys' claimed negligence in failing to properly maintain their rental property in a safe condition (premises liability), ultimately morphed into a criminal investigation to determine not only whether, in fact, murder had been done, but also by what means and who might have been the culprit.

The questions have yet to be definitively or judicially answered—and doubtless never will be—but I am reasonably satisfied that Doug Bynum's death was neither an accident nor, in any way attributable to the Dickeys, both of whom are now deceased. I will be much surprised if the reader will not agree.

One might ask whether Erica's affidavit would not have been sufficient evidence to warrant a criminal prosecution, but it needs to be remembered that her sworn affidavit directly contradicted her earlier sworn testimony on deposition. And, in the absence of any other hard evidence, that fact alone would have created that "reasonable doubt" which would have mandated an acquittal.

I think that I have earlier indicated that Dick Rice had, from time to time, urged me to tell this story, and now that I have done so, I am grateful for his encouragements; I have actually enjoyed the necessary review of my own files, consultations with Dick Rice and Deputy Steve Lord, and, of course, the re-living of that which I have long considered an exceptional case, be it civil, criminal, or an intriguing admixture of the two areas of the law.

I am also greatly appreciative of the efforts of my secretary, Carolyn Benzies, who has patiently and tolerantly suffered through the production of my successive drafts, revisions and re-drafts of this work. I'm quite sure she's worn out and glad to be finally shut of the whole thing.

—John Fulker